The Silent Tide

Book One of The Envoy Chronicles

One

The color came first — always the color — drifting through the suspension like dye released into slow water, and Nia watched it spread across the chamber with the particular attention she had been trained to offer unfamiliar grammars.

It was the First-Speaker who was speaking, and the First-Speaker's chemical signature was cooler than the others', silver-green with undertones of something the Concordance had never settled on a translation for "*patience under weight*," Vance had written in his early notes, though he was also fond of saying that no three English words could do what one Thren phrase did, and that trying to make them was the job. The signature bloomed through the upper volume of the chamber, unfurled across the middle register where humans and Thren shared the room, and sank slowly toward the tiled floor where Nia stood beside the ambassador. She had been inside the suspension for nine days, and by now she could almost tell herself she belonged to it.

The First-Speaker was speaking in all three modes at once, which was the ritual requirement. The vocalization was low enough that Nia felt it in her teeth, water-pitched and bone-conducted, arriving through her skeleton a fraction of a second before it arrived through her ears. The pigment-flash moved along the curve of the First-Speaker's mantle in patterns too fast for Nia to translate in real time. She read the echo, the way a human reading a language they did not yet own read the echo, and the chemical-scent laid the color-argument across the room in long, branching strokes. The three modes were meant to be read as one utterance. In the abstract Nia had known this her entire adult life. In the flesh (which was to say in the suspension, which was to say in this particular warmth around her face and throat) it was still the single most beautiful thing she had ever learned.

Ambassador Vance stood a meter to her left. His hands were folded in the posture of formal attention, palms down, fingers overlapping in the pattern the service called *open hearing*; his bioluminescent translator patch glowed faintly across his sternum in a rhythm Nia had helped calibrate and that still, after nine days, she could not quite read. The patch was a compromise. It rendered his outgoing speech in simplified Thren pigment-glyphs, slow enough for the court to follow and precise enough not to insult anyone by accident, but it could not carry a full sentence. Vance had to do most of the work in his voice and in his face. He had been doing this for eleven years. He was very good at it.

He was also, Nia knew, tired in a way he was not showing. The suspension cost the older body more. He had told her as much on the second day, across the small table in his quarters, with a cup of tea he had not been able to drink because the cup had been too slippery to hold, and he had laughed at himself in a way that had made Nia understand, without being told, that she was being trusted by him. That evening she had gone back to her own quarters and written her first field note that was not about

Thren. *TV is human*, she had written, and then crossed it out, and then circled the crossing-out, and then closed the notebook. The note was still in the notebook. She thought of it now, in the suspension, in the color, in the chamber where the First-Speaker was closing and where she was a junior linguist and where she was also, irrepressibly, someone who had taken the measure of the man beside her and had decided to keep him.

The ninth day of the Acceptance of Speech was structured like a tide that came in slowly and then went out at once. For eight days the Concordance delegation had been arrayed along the lower register of the chamber, receiving (that was the correct verb in Thren, though the Concordance had been quietly translating it as *listening* for a decade) the rehearsed address of each Current in turn. On the ninth day the First Current made the closing, and then the delegation itself was permitted to answer in a single prepared utterance. If the answer was received, the trade provisions would pass into the next week. If it was not, everyone would go home. There was a third possibility, which the junior diplomats did not like to name and the senior diplomats had never once, in Nia's hearing, described aloud: that the answer would be received imperfectly, and the peace would go on, and the trade provisions would not. This possibility, which looked like a tie, was actually a slow loss.

Nia's job on the ninth day was specific and small. She was to stand at Vance's right hand side, and she was to watch the Thren chemical register for any drift from the expected signatures. She was to touch the back of his hand twice if anything went wrong. That was the whole of it. In eight prior days she had not touched his hand once.

In the middle register of the chamber, above the First-Speaker's silver-green color and beneath the soft yellow drifting down from the upper volume, a small shape was beginning to form.

Nia noticed it the way one notices a bird at the edge of a field. First, as movement, second as grammar. It did not belong to the First-Speaker; it was too warm in its base, too rounded in its edges. She parsed it reflexively as *Fourth Current register, scholar's pitch, unscheduled* and her eye tracked it up and across the volume until it resolved into a body.

It was a Thren she had seen before. He was standing in the recessed alcove of the second tier, not among the speakers and not among the observers, in the place that belonged to scholars who had come because they had a question and not because they had been summoned. His limbs were held in the posture of *attending at an angle*, which was polite but not participatory. His signature was small, careful, insistent. He was looking at her.

She had registered him on the third day of the ceremony, when he had spoken, briefly and without introduction, inside a long interval during which a servant of the Sixth Current had sung a water-poem that Nia had half-understood. He had said something about language that was not protocol, and that she had not been able to reply to. She had written his signature in the margin of her notes and had not, afterward, been able to find out his name.

He was looking at her now with the chemical equivalent of a held breath.

Nia returned her attention to the First-Speaker.

The First-Speaker closed her color-argument with a downward fall, the pigment trailing through the lower register like a breath let go, and the chamber entered what the protocol called the *half-beat*, the silence-that-was-not-silence in which the receiver of the speech composed their answer. In human communication this silence was often a second or two. In Thren, it could be thirty seconds or more, and the Thren did not call it silence. They called it the part of the speech that had not yet been spoken.

Vance turned his head one degree toward Nia, which was the pre-arranged signal that he was about to begin, and Nia tightened her shoulders one millimeter, which was the pre-arranged acknowledgment. She did not touch his hand.

That was when she saw the new color.

It arrived in the upper volume of the chamber, above and behind the First-Speaker's last silver-green fall, and for a long half-second it did not register as anything she needed to attend to. The Thren court was wide. Extraneous signatures drifted through a chamber all the time, from servants, from low-level attendants, or from the ambient breathing of minor speakers in the tiers. She had been trained to filter them. She had not filtered this one.

It was the wrong shape.

It was not in the wrong place or the wrong register, those she would have caught sooner. It was in the wrong *shape*. Thren chemical speech unfolded the way a vine grew, forked, uneven, reaching in three directions for every one it withdrew. This color unfolded the way a sentence diagrammed on a blackboard unfolded. It had symmetry. It had the spacing of a paragraph. It was beautiful the way a line of type was beautiful, which is to say not at all, which is to say the wrong kind of beautiful, the kind that did not belong inside a living register.

Nia's professional half leaned forward. She had spent her entire adult life looking for new registers. She thought, distinctly: *this is something I have never seen.*

She thought it for longer than she should have.

Vance coughed once, very quietly, and Nia's professional half was still reading the shape when her private half realized that the color had reached him. It had reached him because it had been released close enough to his face that it would reach him first. It was beautiful and it was wrong, and it was on his lungs.

The patch across his sternum flickered in a sequence that was not one of the calibrated sequences.

Nia touched his hand.

She had been trained to touch his hand twice. She touched it once, because it had fallen away from hers immediately.

The color that had killed Vance did not stop when he stopped. It continued its diagram across the upper volume, the way a sentence continues until it reaches its period, and the period was the small, wet, terrible sound that Ambassador Teodoro Vance made as his body entered the suspension in a way it was not meant to enter.

Nia caught him.

It was not a catching in any real sense. The suspension caught him first; she only guided. His weight went through her hands and down, and she went down with him, knees and then hips and then the flat of her braced palm against the tile, and the suspension took him as the suspension took any body; forgivingly, resistantly, never entirely still. His eyes were open. His eyes were still Vance's. For three seconds Nia believed, in the way one believes something one has decided in advance, that she would be able to reach him through the patch, and she opened her own mouth to try, and the suspension came into her mouth instead, and she tasted the color.

It tasted the way a forgery looked. Clean. Empty of where it had come from. She would remember the taste for the rest of her life, and she would never describe it to anyone, because to describe it would be to give it a register it did not deserve.

Above her, the chamber was entering a state she had studied but never seen. The First-Speaker, in the upper tier, had folded her three channels into a single shape Nia did not know. The Fourth Current scholar in the alcove (the one who had been looking at her) was no longer looking at her. He was looking at the color, and his own signature had gone out like a candle. Around the middle register the other Currents were retreating inward, their pigments pulling close to their bodies, the chamber going dark the way a pool goes dark when every fish in it decides, at once, to sink. This was the Thren response to a violation of speech. Nia had read about it in three different textbooks, none of which had prepared her to see it while kneeling on the tile with Vance's head against her thigh.

A voice she did not know, human, behind her, Concordance, said her name. Another voice said *get her up.* Another voice said *do not drain the suspension yet*, and then, after a beat, *drain it.*

The suspension began to fall.

It fell the way the Thren had engineered it to fall in the case of a breach, slowly, from the upper volume first, the warmth withdrawing in a plane across her face and then across her shoulders and then her chest. As it withdrew it took the color with it, the beautiful symmetrical wrong color and the silver-green fall of the First-Speaker and the remnants of eight days of speech, all of it siphoned into the recovery mantle below the tile where it could be read later. Someone would read it. Nia, in some part of herself she would not reach for days, understood that she was one of the people who would have to read it.

When the suspension had fallen to her waist she let herself look up. The chamber was in ritual silence. It was not the silence of the half-beat; it was the older silence, the one the textbooks translated as *the speech that will not be spoken.* Every Thren in the tiers had folded into the posture of withdrawn hearing. Every color in the room had died. The Fourth Current scholar in the alcove had closed his eyes.

Hands came under Nia's arms. She let them.

Vance was carried out of the suspension before she was. She was told, later, that this was protocol. She was told many things later.

The last thing she was aware of, before the chamber doors opened and the corridor beyond it resolved into something she could walk in, was the small and shameful fact that her professional half was still, even now, trying to finish reading the color. She let it finish. It was the last service she would render him.

The color said: *I am speech.*

The color was a lie, and Vance was dead, and Nia had spent her one half-second on the lie.

She would not, in the whole of her life afterward, get that half-second back.

Two

The corridor was dry.

That was the first thing Nia understood outside the suspension, and the understanding arrived the way news arrives, from a long way off. Her clothes were not wet. The suspension left nothing on the skin when it drained; it was engineered not to, because the chemical residues would carry speech out of the chamber where speech was not meant to go. She stood in the corridor in the clothes she had walked into the chamber in, and her hair was not wet, and the color was gone, and the sound was gone, and the pressure around her face was gone, and she could hear herself breathing.

She could hear her breathing because the corridor was a standard-atmosphere volume with hard walls, and sound moved through it the way sound was supposed to move. Each breath arrived sharp and fast and entered her ears through one channel only. She had forgotten, in nine days, how thin her breathing sounded in air.

Someone was beside her. She was being walked.

The person at her elbow was from the embassy security detail, a woman whose name Nia had learned on day two and had lost by the next hour. She did not ask for it again. It seemed important, right now, to ask nothing.

The corridor emptied into the air-lock atrium, and the atrium emptied into the Concordance compound proper. The Concordance compound was a clean interior of panels and lights and quiet machinery humming at a frequency that had nothing to do with bone. Nia walked through it. She knew where she was going because she had been here for nine days. She was going to the embassy, which was also where she lived, which was also where her quarters were. The woman at her elbow turned her to the left and then to the right, and Nia went where she was turned.

Someone had run ahead. The door of her quarters was already open when she reached it.

Adrian was inside.

She did not know how he had gotten word. She did not know how he had gotten here. He was on the delegation with her, a senior exobiologist specializing in Thren chemical communication, who had come to Sepharu three weeks ahead of the main party to set up the research wing's reference catalogue. She had seen him on the second day for tea. She had seen him again on the fifth day for a short walk in the compound garden, which was a lawn of kept Terran grass under a sun lamp, and they had talked about nothing in particular and he had called her Nee the way he had always called her Nee, and it had made her feel, for an hour, that she had a prior life.

He was sitting on the low bench by the door. He stood when she came in.

He did not say anything. He did not try to. He crossed the room and took the towel that was folded on the dresser and held it out to her, which was the right thing to do, because though the suspension had left her dry her palms were pressing wet against her thighs without her permission, and the towel was the only explanation for them that she was able to accept.

She took the towel. She did not dry her hands with it. She held it.

"You should sit," he said.

She sat.

Adrian Cho was six years older than she was, which she had found important at twenty-four and stopped finding important at twenty-six. He had a long face, a patient mouth, and hair he had worn short since the year after his doctorate, when the suspension wing he was going to be working under had told him in polite terms that hair was a liability in water-volume research. He had kept it short, even after he had moved out of water-volume research. By now it was a choice, not a rule. Everything about him was like that; a thing he had once done for a reason and kept doing because he had forgotten how to reconsider. She had told him so once, across a table at the academy, when they had still been each other's, and he had laughed the way he laughed when he wanted to be annoyed at a true thing, but had not changed anything about himself.

He was kneeling in front of her now. He had kept his distance.

"Nee," he said.

"He's dead," Nia said. Her voice arrived in the room at a volume she had not authorized. It was much louder than it should have been.

"I know," Adrian said.

"He was talking," she said.

"I know."

"I was watching the color. I was reading it. I was reading it as Thren."

He did not move. He had always been very still when she was not. She thought, dimly, that this was one of the things that had made them good together for the length of time that they had been good together.

"The poison was structured like speech," she said. "It came in like chemical speech. I was parsing it. I didn't move."

"Okay," Adrian said.

"I had half a second."

"Okay."

"I didn't move."

Adrian did not correct her. He did not tell her that half a second was not enough time to move. He did not tell her that no one on her training committee had ever stopped a toxin in the suspension in less than a full second. He did not tell her that the patch had not flickered the warning sequence, that Vance had not touched her hand to signal, that the fault was not hers. He was very good at not telling her things.

He reached out and closed his hand around her wrist, just above where her fingers were wrapped around the towel, and he held it there, and did not move it.

She cried for the first time since the chamber.

She cried the way a person cries who has been taught to read, which is to say not usefully. She was still parsing. She was parsing her own breathing. She was parsing the way Adrian's hand felt on her wrist, which was steady and warm and very slightly calloused across the second knuckle, and she was thinking, somewhere behind her grief, that the chemical-scent register of a sentence like this one would be silver-gold, would bloom slowly, would drift in the upper volume of a room and settle toward the floor. She would not tell him this. She would never tell anyone this. It was the only private sentence she had left.

Her comm chirped once, paused, chirped a second time, and went silent.

"That'll be the civil service," Adrian said.

"What do they want?"

"A statement. Or to tell you not to give a statement. One of the two."

"Which?"

"It'll be both, tonight, from different offices, about forty minutes apart."

She nodded. She was nodding at the towel in her lap. The towel was folded the way the embassy laundry folded towels, in thirds, with the embossed seal of the Concordance on the top layer. She had not noticed the seal for nine days. She noticed it now.

"Eat," Adrian said.

"I can't."

"Eat anyway."

He got up. He did something in the small galley alcove that involved water and the sound of a kettle and the unsealing of a wrap. She did not watch him. She watched the ceiling, which was a panel of light diffused to resemble sky, which it did not, and which was running on the evening cycle now because the compound had been running on the evening cycle for ninety minutes. The ninth day of ceremony had not ended on time. Ceremonies on Sepharu were scheduled to break an hour before the compound's local dusk. This one had broken seven minutes after the First-Speaker's last fall, and the last fall had been roughly three minutes into the protocol half-beat, and Vance had been dead for, she did not want to count, she counted, forty-one minutes.

When she was twenty-three, two years into her doctoral work, her advisor had brought her into a small room with cream-colored walls and had handed her a set of phones and a data slate with a single forty-second recording on it. This was a Thren utterance, her advisor had said, in three channels simultaneously, captured by a buoy, cleaned, synced, rendered playable by a human nervous system through a translation that was accurate in structure if not in feel. Nia had put on the phones. She had watched the pigment-flash render on the slate screen and she had smelled, through a small vial her advisor handed her at the eight-second mark, the chemical register folded down into a simulation of a human olfactory signal. The recording had been a greeting. It had been the first greeting transmitted to a human ship in Thren. Nia had listened to it once, and then she had listened to it again, and then she had removed the phones and walked out of the room and down the corridor and into the bathroom at the end of the hall, and she had stood for twenty minutes with her hands on the porcelain of the sink. She had understood what her life was going to be.

She had understood it and she had been happy.

That was the part she would never, after tonight, be able to hold in her mind without the other part attached.

"Here," Adrian said.

He set a cup on the low table by her chair. It was tea. It was the kind he made, which was the kind he had been making since the academy, bitter black with a pinch of salt at the bottom. She lifted it with both hands because one hand alone would have shaken. She drank.

"The Thren are not talking," he said, quietly. "To us, I mean. They closed the audience chamber at the second bell and the First Current has been in silence since. The Third Current has requested isolation, which means they're going into the sealed meditation volumes for some number of hours. The Fourth Current hasn't said anything at all, which is what the Fourth Current does when there's nothing it wants to be held to."

"The Sixth?"

"Grieving, quietly. Formally."

"The Seventh?"

"Nobody can find the Seventh."

She nodded. She drank.

"And us?" she said.

"The senior diplomats are drafting. HQ is waking up about now, so expect traffic. Dhillon is acting head of delegation until we hear from the Chair. The civil service wants a clean story by morning."

"What story."

"Any clean one. That's the shape of it."

"A Thren did it."

"That's what they'd like the story to be, yes."

"A Thren didn't."

He did not answer. He did not need to. He had been on the delegation for three weeks before her and had spent the first two of them in the Sepharu research wing, working on a chemical catalogue she had helped him reference, and he knew as well as she did that the shape of a Thren chemical message did not match the shape of what had killed Vance. He had not said so, and he would not, probably, tonight. That was the civil service's problem.

"I can't sleep," Nia said.

"I didn't ask you to," he said.

He sat on the floor at the foot of her chair. He did not hold her. He did not touch her. He was there, and he would be there in the morning. She understood, with a gratitude she would not be able to feel properly until two days later, that he had rearranged his evening to be here.

The panel above her ran through to full dusk, and then slowly, minute by minute, to the sleep cycle, which was a deep cold dark that the embassy designers had calibrated to approximate Earth winter night. Nia did not sleep. She lay on the couch, because Adrian had insisted, and she did not sleep, and she watched the simulated sky go dark, and she replayed the half-second, again and again, and she watched the color unfold in her mind the way it had unfolded in the chamber. Each time she watched it she understood one more small thing about what it was and who had made it and what would have to happen now.

By the time the sleep cycle had deepened to its true dark, she had understood enough to be afraid.

She stayed awake.

Three

The first chime of the morning cycle sounded at 05:42 local, and Nia heard it the way a person hears a knock on a door she had been expecting and hoping would not come.

She had not slept.

She sat up on the couch. The blanket someone had draped over her at some hour she had not registered slid down to her lap. The room was warm, which the embassy engineers had decided was the correct temperature for a human body recovering from suspension exposure. Nia had never read the internal manuals on this. She knew the temperature because she had been trained in it. Everything about the compound had been designed to keep the human body inside a small envelope of conditions that were not Sepharu. It was the most comforting thing in the room, and she could not bear any of it.

Adrian was gone.

His coat was over the back of the chair by the door, which meant he had not gone far. There was a note folded on the low table, weighted by the tea cup from the night before. She would read it later.

The comm on her wrist pulsed quietly. One of the civil service offices had been sending messages since 04:00. She cleared her screen and did not read those either.

She stood. She stayed standing for long enough to understand that she could. Then she went into the small bathroom. She washed her face and the back of her neck with water that was too cold, then too hot, then the correct temperature. The mirror was designed to read a human face and flatter it, which the embassy designers had also decided was the correct policy. The face in the mirror did not look flattered. It looked like a person who had, at some point during the night, stopped being twenty-four and thirty-one both at once, and had become a third age she did not have a number for.

Behind the face in the mirror, the word came. Forgery.

The word had been waiting for her since the half-beat. She had not let it arrive in so many letters last night. She let it arrive now.

The color that had killed Vance had been a forgery. She had thought so while kneeling on the tile. She had thought so through the tea. She had thought so lying on the couch watching the sleep cycle dim. She had not said it aloud. She did not say it aloud now.

She dried her face.

Adrian had left a note. He was at the research wing. Dhillon wanted her by seven. She was to eat something. She was not to sign anything. He had signed it Love, A.

Nia read it twice. She folded the note into thirds, which was the way she folded everything now, and put it in the inner pocket of the robe hanging on the hook by the door. She did not eat. She put water in a cup. She drank it. She refilled the cup and drank that. She dressed.

The Concordance compound at 06:15 in the morning was a quiet building with a low hum that came from the air system and a second quieter hum that came from the gate relay in the basement. The corridor to the senior civil service offices ran along the eastern exterior wall, which on Sepharu was always the side the sun did not reach, because Sepharu had an odd rotation the compound had been oriented not to fight. Nia walked it at 06:48. She passed three junior staff who did not look at her and one senior clerk who did.

A news panel at the junction was running the overnight feed on mute, its ticker scrolling middle-range stories through the lower third of the screen. Nia's eye caught one as it passed. A mining crew on a deep-field extraction platform had been found unresponsive at shift change. Six alive and breathing. None of them responsive to light or sound. Preliminary cause atmospheric contamination, no confirmed agent. The ticker moved on. Nia kept walking.

The clerk was a woman named Adaeze Okonkwo. She had processed Nia's arrival papers nine days before. She had smiled at Nia then, warmly and briefly, the way people smile when they recognize a shared second language. Adaeze did not smile now. She looked at Nia with a kind of professional concern, and then looked away, which was the service's way of telling her the conversation inside was not going to be what she expected.

Dhillon's outer door opened on its own.

He was sitting at the round table he kept in the outer room for meetings he wanted to treat as conversations, which was therefore a tell that he did not want this one to be a conversation. There were two other people with him. One was a woman Nia had seen once at the gate arrival who had identified herself as legal counsel, and whose name Nia had filed and lost. The other was a man Nia did not know at all, dressed in the unassertive charcoal of the civil service, holding a dataslate in the posture of someone who was going to read from it.

"Dr. Okafor-Reyes," Dhillon said. He stood, which was kind. He gestured her to a chair.

She took it.

"I'm sorry," Dhillon said. "I'm sorry on behalf of the service, and I'm sorry in person. Teodoro was a friend. I will not pretend he was not."

"Thank you," Nia said.

"We have to take a statement from you."

"Yes."

"For the record, and for the Thren record, and for the Parliament once they convene. I want to be clear about what I'm asking for before I ask it."

"Yes."

"I need you to tell me what you saw."

"Yes."

"And I need you to tell me how to read it."

Nia did not answer.

The legal counsel woman had not looked up from her slate. The man in charcoal had his index finger held above the record function on his own, waiting. Dhillon saw Nia not answer. The two lines at the corners of his mouth settled a small further fraction of a millimeter, the way a man's face settles when he has confirmed something he had been afraid of.

"The preliminary chemical analysis is in," he said.

"I'd like to see it."

"You will. I want to talk through it with you first."

"All right."

"The structure of the poisoning agent is consistent with a Thren chemical signature from the Fifth Current."

Nia, who had been about to accept a glass of water from the carafe on the table, set the glass down.

"Consistent with," Dhillon said, "is the phrasing we have. The preliminary report uses the word analogous. The senior chemist at the Sepharu research wing signed off on it at 03:40 this morning. She has been up most of the night. Her report identifies seven structural features of the agent and matches them to seven known features of Fifth Current aggression-register chemistry. Her report is thorough. It is cautious. It is the first thing the Parliament will see."

"Adrian signed off on this?"

Dhillon hesitated for half a second he had not intended.

"No," he said. "Dr. Cho was not asked."

"Why."

"Because Dr. Cho is your partner. Former."

"Former."

"He declared a prior relationship on his onboarding forms. The service is careful about this."

"The senior chemist is not Adrian."

"Correct."

"Who is the senior chemist."

"Dr. Tamar Halpern-Ødegård. She flew in four weeks ago on a short-rotation assignment."

"Four weeks ago."

"Yes."

Nia did not say what she was thinking. She had never met Dr. Halpern-Ødegård. She had seen her name once, on a duty roster on day three. She had assumed she was part of the extended research staff, not central to any ongoing question. Four weeks, in Concordance civil service terms, was a rotation short enough to be anomalous. Long-rotation specialists stayed for six months at minimum.

She looked at Dhillon. Dhillon, who was very good at his job, had not moved.

"Have the Thren been shown this report," Nia said.

"Not yet."

"Don't."

"That's not my decision to make, Doctor."

"Whose is it."

"The Chair's."

"The Chair hasn't convened yet."

"The Chair is awake."

"The Chair is a caretaker."

"The Chair is the Chair."

Nia breathed out through her nose. She looked at the legal counsel woman, who had looked up now. She looked at the man in charcoal, who had thumbed his slate to record without her noticing. She looked at Dhillon, who had let him.

"I need to see the chemical analysis before I give a statement," she said.

"You can have it in an hour."

"I need to see it now."

"I can't—"

"Then I won't give a statement now."

Dhillon did not sigh. Dhillon, in thirty years of civil service, had trained himself out of sighing. But the quality of his not-sighing was very specific in this moment, and Nia read it as clearly as if he had sighed aloud. He was going to give her the analysis. He was going to give it to her because he needed her. And he was going to make her wait for it by a small margin, because he needed the record to show that he had been careful.

"An hour," he said.

"An hour."

She left his office at 07:14.

The corridor was the same corridor she had walked in. Adaeze Okonkwo was no longer at her station. The junior staff had thickened in number by three, and they were not making eye contact with her in a more organized way than they had been twenty-five minutes ago. Nia registered this. She did not react. She walked to the small atrium at the junction of the civil service wing and the residential wing. She sat on one of the benches the embassy had installed because the architects had believed human diplomats needed to sit down occasionally. They had been correct.

She had an hour.

She opened her comm. She did not read the messages. She opened her private notes, which she had been keeping since her doctoral work and which she did not keep in a form the civil service could subpoena, because her advisor had taught her not to. She wrote three lines.

Fifth Current aggression register is not how chemical speech kills.

The structure was wrong in the direction of simple, not wrong in the direction of Thren.

Halpern-Ødegård.

She closed the notes.

Her comm pulsed once, not an incoming message but the softer pulse that meant a proximity prompt. She looked down.

A Thren was in the atrium.

He was standing on the visitor side of the low glass partition that divided the atrium from the garden beyond, which was where the compound permitted Thren to enter without passing through the air-lock into human atmosphere. He was dressed in the ceremonial collars of his Current, which was a costume a Thren wore to an audience, not to a chance encounter with a human on a bench at seven-seventeen in the morning. His limbs were held in attending at an angle. His signature was small and very careful. He had thinned it to the edge of what could still be called speech.

Nia did not stand.

She looked at him across the glass. He looked at her across the glass.

After a moment he lifted one of his forward limbs and placed the flat of it against the glass. The pigment on the underside of that limb was doing a thing Nia had never seen a Thren limb do in a public space. It was cycling, slowly, through a pattern of four signatures she recognized from the chamber the night before. The First-Speaker's silver-green. The ritual silence of withdrawn hearing. The Sixth Current's formal grief. And a fourth signature, very small, that she knew immediately, because it was the residual signal from Vance's translator patch in the last half-second before the patch had stopped.

Vorathan was showing her, in a Thren public space, through glass, that he had read what had killed Vance. That he had been reading it last night in the alcove while everyone else had folded. That he knew what the signature had been carrying.

He was also, in the showing, telling her something the Thren court was not yet telling the Concordance.

Nia rose from the bench. She did not cross to the glass. She crossed two steps toward it, enough that anyone watching through an embassy camera would register movement, not contact. She held her right hand up at her side, fingers spread in the gesture the service called listening-to-learn.

Vorathan's pigment pattern cycled once more. Then his limb dropped.

He walked away through the garden.

Nia watched him go. She sat back down on the bench.

He had come in ceremonial collars.

She understood only now that the collars were not a costume at all. They were a shield. He had presented himself in his Current's formal dress so that if he were seen approaching the human side of the glass, no Thren watching could claim he had done so casually. He had come dressed as a Fourth Current scholar on official business. He had conducted five seconds of official business through a glass partition. In those five seconds he had told her that he had seen what had killed Vance, and that the Fourth Current had not been told to see it.

He was going to pay for this.

Nia pressed her hand to her forehead. She sat there for longer than she had intended. Then she got up, and she walked back toward Dhillon's office. Her hour was not up. She was going to take what she had. She was going to take what she had just been given. She was going to go in early.

She was going to read the chemical analysis. She was going to read it carefully. And then she was going to refuse to sign it.

Four

The outer room was empty when Nia came back.

The legal counsel woman was gone. The man in charcoal was gone. Dhillon was sitting alone at the round table, the dataslate still in front of him, a fresh cup of coffee at his elbow he had not touched. He looked up when she walked in. He did not seem surprised she had come back early.

"You didn't take the hour," he said.

"I don't need the hour," Nia said.

She sat down across from him. She pulled the slate toward her. She turned it on.

"Dr. Okafor-Reyes—"

"I'm reading it, Dhillon."

He closed his mouth. He watched her read.

The report was seven pages long, written by a person who had been awake for most of eighteen hours. Nia could see the fatigue in the syntax, which was a thing her graduate advisor had taught her to read, and had told her was one of the few useful forensic skills a linguist had. Halpern-Ødegård's sentences went short in the second half of the document, in the way sentences went short when a writer was no longer choosing short sentences on purpose. Her conclusions were hedged with two kinds of hedges: the kind a scientist used when she knew she was speaking above her evidence, and the kind a scientist used when she had been told to. Nia could not tell which was which. She could tell they were both present.

The chemical agent had seven features. Each of the seven had an analogue in Fifth Current aggression-register chemistry. The agent was, therefore, analogous to Fifth Current aggression.

The report did not mention that the agent also had thirteen features that did not have an analogue anywhere in Thren chemical literature. It did not mention that Fifth Current aggression-register chemistry, where it was documented, almost never appeared in any vector that could cross into human lungs. It did not mention that the seven matching features were the seven most commonly cited in the public literature, the features a researcher would find if she studied Thren chemistry from library papers and not from field recordings.

The report was not a forgery the way the poison was a forgery. It was only a forgery of what it pretended to be. It was competent, cautious, and designed to pass.

Nia closed the slate.

"I'm not going to sign a statement consistent with this report," she said.

"I haven't asked you to."

"You're going to."

"Yes."

"I won't."

Dhillon looked at her for a long moment. He reached for the coffee at his elbow and drank half of it cold. He set the cup down carefully. He had very good hands, Nia had noticed on day three. She had noticed because she had been noticing everything, and because she had been trying to decide whether Dhillon was a person who would help her or a person who would appear to help her.

"The Chair wants this closed by end of day local," he said.

"The Chair is a caretaker."

"You said that before."

"It was true before."

"The Chair has been on a call with HQ for four hours. HQ is not a caretaker."

Nia did not answer.

"I am asking you for a statement," Dhillon said. "I am not asking you to sign off on this report. I am asking you to tell me what you saw, in the words you would use to tell any of your peers, and to let me decide what of that can be put on the record tonight."

"You will put all of it on the record that serves the report."

"That is my job."

"Then I won't give the statement."

He nodded. He had expected this. He looked tired in a way she had not seen a civil servant look tired before, which was the particular tired of a man who had decided to do his job well inside a system that was not going to let him.

"I am going to have to ask you to remain in your quarters until we have further guidance," he said.

"For my welfare."

"For your welfare."

"Under guard."

"The service does not call it a guard, Doctor."

"I know what the service calls it."

"I know you do."

She got up. He did not stand. She walked to the door, opened it, and looked back at him once. She understood, with a clarity she would want to remember later, that Dhillon had given her something in this conversation he had not been asked to give. He had let her read the report. He had let her read it without the legal counsel in the room. He had let her see what was missing from it. He had not told her what to do with what she saw; he had only told her what would happen if she did nothing.

He was already a better man than the civil service would let him be.

She closed the door.

The corridor back to her quarters had a junior officer in it now who had not been in it earlier, walking behind her at the correct distance to be called an escort and the correct distance to be called a coincidence. Nia did not look at him. She walked at her usual pace. She reached the door of her quarters, used her own access, and went inside.

Adrian was waiting for her.

He was sitting in the chair by the window. He had not taken off his coat. He looked up when she came in, and the look on his face was the look of a man who had been rehearsing what he was going to say and had just lost all the rehearsal.

"Nee," he said.

"Adrian."

"How did it go."

"You know how it went."

"I heard some. I want to hear it from you."

She put her comm on the table by the door. She took off her shoes. She sat on the couch she had not slept on, and she looked at him across the space of the room, and she noticed the thing she had noticed last night, which was that he was being very still.

"They want the Fifth Current," she said.

"I heard."

"The report is bad."

"Bad how."

"Bad like a student essay. Bad like someone wrote it at the library."

He was quiet.

"Halpern-Ødegård is a short-rotation specialist," Nia said. "Four weeks. Has anyone else on the delegation met her?"

Adrian took longer to answer than the question required. It was half a beat. It was a beat Nia would not have caught yesterday.

"I met her once," he said. "At a lunch in the research wing. Three weeks ago. She's competent."

"Is she."

"She's… yes. Yes, she's competent."

"Would she write this report?"

He did not answer at once.

"Adrian."

"I think she would write this report if someone asked her to in the right way. I also think she'd believe it while she was writing it. That's the shape of her work."

"Who asked her?"

"I don't know."

"Who asked her, Adrian."

"Nee, I don't know."

She watched him. He was holding himself too carefully. He was a man who held himself too carefully when he was tired. He had been up all night. She had spent enough years of her life reading him to know that this was not tired. It was something else. It was a shape she had read on him twice in her life. The first had been the afternoon he had told her his postdoc was moving him to Ceres, which had been the afternoon they had ended. The second had been the morning she had asked him, years later, whether he was happy.

She did not let her face say what she was reading.

"You should go," she said.

"Nee—"

"I mean it. I need to sleep. I can't do that while you're here."

"Okay."

He stood. He came to the couch, bent down, and kissed the top of her head, which was a thing he had done sometimes at the academy on mornings when she had been up all night studying. He stayed there for longer than he had to. Then he straightened.

"I'm at the research wing through dinner," he said. "Then my quarters. Call me."

"I will."

"Nee."

"I will. Go."

He went.

She listened to his steps in the corridor outside her door. She listened to the junior officer's steps adjusting as Adrian passed him. She listened to the steps fade to the junction, and down into the compound where she could not hear them.

She sat on the couch for three minutes.

Then she got up.

She went to the small desk in the alcove off her quarters. She sat down. She turned on the secure terminal the service had given her on day one. She logged in with her junior-linguist credentials. She opened the request form for the suspension recordings.

She was a junior linguist assigned to the delegation. The recordings from the chamber were available to junior linguists for professional review. The form had three fields. Reason. Scope. Duration.

She filled them in. Reason: independent verification of preliminary chemical analysis, consistent with standing scholarly practice. Scope: full nine-day ceremony, all channels, all tiers. Duration: forty-eight hours, renewable.

She submitted the form.

She closed the terminal. She sat in the chair. She waited.

It would take the service between two minutes and forty minutes to either approve the request automatically or flag it for review. She had worded it the way a scholar would have worded it on any previous project. She had worded it so refusing it would be the anomaly. Refusing it would leave a paper trail. Refusing it would require someone in the civil service to put a name to the refusal.

The terminal pinged at the seven-minute mark.

The request was approved.

She sat for another full minute, letting herself feel what she was about to do.

Then she opened the files.

The suspension recordings were organized by tier and channel. She found the ninth day. She found the half-beat. She found the volume of the chamber in the seconds before and after the color had arrived in the upper register. She isolated the channel she wanted, the chemical-scent layer, the layer that had killed Vance.

She put on the phones. She put on the olfactory simulator.

She started listening.

Five

The first thing she heard on the record was her own breath.

The suspension had been engineered to capture every chemical signal released into its volume. That was, after all, the point of it. Her breath had been one of those signals. So had Vance's. So had the breath of every human, every Thren, and every attending servant inside the chamber on every day of the ceremony. She had forgotten, in the nine days, that her own breathing had been recorded. She had forgotten it the way one forgets one's own face in a photograph one is inside of.

She paused the playback at the first second. She took the phones off, staring into the distance. She contemplated putting everything down and falling into a dreamless sleep. She put the phones on again.

The recording was a reconstruction, not an experience. The embassy's playback tools rendered the chamber's color onto the slate screen in layered pigment strokes a trained linguist could read. They rendered the chemical layer as a scented air fed through a close-fit simulator, released in timed pulses that approximated the dispersal pattern of the original signal. They rendered the bone-conducted vocalization as a tactile signal through the cushion of the chair she was sitting in, which pulsed under her thighs in slow, irregular beats that were very nearly the real thing. It was not the suspension. It was a technical reproduction of the suspension, which was to say a version of the suspension a human body could review without drowning in it.

It was also a ghost.

She let herself sit inside the ghost for thirty seconds. She had not planned to. She was listening to the start of the ninth day, before the First-Speaker had begun to speak, when the chamber had gone quiet in the specific way a Thren chamber went quiet before a ceremony. She could hear Vance breathing. She could hear herself breathing. She could hear, at a lower register, the three attendants of the Fourth Current tier moving softly in the upper alcoves. One of those attendants had been Vorathan.

She began to time-stamp.

She advanced through the recording in the practiced skip-and-settle of a linguist working a document. She let the First-Speaker's address play in its entirety, not because she needed to, but because the professional training that had kept her upright through last night's chair also kept her honest now: you did not analyze a speech by cutting straight to its interruption. You heard the speech first.

The First-Speaker had been beautiful. Nia let her be beautiful. She closed her eyes at the point in the closing where the silver-green had fallen through the lower register, and she felt the fall in her chair, and she did not cry, though she would have in a kinder room.

She came to the half-beat.

Before she slowed the playback, she did something she had not planned to do. She let the last seconds of the half-beat play at full speed.

The color reached Vance before Nia had thought it had. That was the first thing she saw. The chamber volume was wide, and she had believed, the night before, that the color had moved through the upper volume for a full second before reaching his face. It had not. It had been released close enough to his face that the first branch of its unfolding had met his mouth on the inhale. The forger had known where Vance would be standing. The forger had measured the release.

Vance coughed at 17:42:41.3 local. Nia marked the time-stamp. His patch flickered at 17:42:41.6. Nia's own body turned toward him at 17:42:42.0, which was the half-second she would remember for the rest of her life. It was also the half-second she had spent, she could see now, watching the color instead of the man.

She watched her past self reach for his hand.

She watched her past self get there one beat after the hand had stopped being a hand she could reach.

She watched her past self go down with the body.

The recording caught her breath at the kneel. She was not going to analyze her own breath. She moved the time-stamp past it.

She slowed the playback to a quarter speed.

The half-beat had lasted three minutes before Vance fell. She had registered it as long in real time. On the record it was longer still. She let the three minutes play. She watched the color map on the slate, which showed the chamber's volume as a cube rendered in shifting strata. She could see the residue of the First-Speaker's silver-green settling toward the tile. She could see the soft yellow of the upper volume. She could see, in the uppermost alcove where the scholars sat, a single thin thread of Vorathan's signature held in attending at an angle. She could see the cube's southwest corner where a small, patient, careful release had begun.

There.

She marked the time-stamp. She zoomed on the southwest upper volume. She increased the color sensitivity of the slate. She slowed the playback further, to a tenth speed.

The color arrived.

It arrived the way she remembered, because the way she remembered had been the correct way. It unfolded symmetrically, branched at regular intervals, spaced itself across the upper volume like a line of type on a page. It did exactly what she had seen it do. She watched it unfold four times at tenth speed. On the fourth watch, she understood something she had not understood in the chamber. The symmetry was not only wrong. It was clever. The forger had chosen seven features of Thren chemistry to reproduce, and had arranged those seven features in a pattern that cited the Fifth Current's aggression register without quite using it. It was not a copy of Fifth Current speech. It was a pastiche of Fifth Current speech designed to pass at a first reading, and to hold up under a second, provided the second reading was also cursory.

It would not hold up under a third.

Nia, on what was her roughly fifth reading by now, was watching it fail.

She pulled up the Thren chemistry reference database, which was a curated catalogue of every Thren chemical-speech signature the Concordance had documented in the eleven years of contact. She ran a similarity search on the seven matching features. The database returned a ranked list of source papers. She read the top ten.

All of them were published. All of them were in translation. All of them were from the kind of broad-survey reference literature a human scholar would reach for in her first year of study of Thren chemistry. None was from the narrower specialist papers where Fifth Current aggression register was actually described in the field. The forger had not read those. The forger had read the library copy.

It was, Nia thought, the kind of mistake a very careful graduate student would have made.

She ran the similarity search against the thirteen non-matching features. The database returned no results.

She stopped. She stared at the blank return. She ran the search again, widening the parameters. The database returned no results.

The thirteen features were not Thren.

Which meant, Nia understood, that they were something else. They were engineered. They had been built to carry the other seven. They were the scaffolding. The seven features were the signage. The whole structure was a piece of architecture dressed up as a piece of language.

She needed a chemist.

She closed the terminal. She removed the olfactory simulator. She put her hands flat on the desk and sat very still.

The natural next move was Adrian. Adrian was the only chemist on the delegation who was not asleep and who was not Halpern-Ødegård. Adrian had a doctorate in Thren chemical communication, which was the exact field she needed. Adrian was also the person she had been reading on the couch two hours earlier, and the thing she had read on him had not gone away.

She made herself think about this.

The thing she had read on him was a stillness she had read on him twice before. Both previous times had been moments when he was holding something he did not want to say. That was not, in itself, evidence. A man in his position last night might be holding all sorts of things and saying none of them. She was a person who was watched. He was a person watching her. It was possible the stillness was only that.

It was also possible that it was not.

She sat with this for two minutes. At the end of the two minutes she understood something about herself she did not like. She had been trained to name what she saw. She had been trained to name it in the Thren modalities, in the human modalities, across the registers of translation, at the level of syntax, at the level of pragmatics, at every level the language arts had given her. And she was, in this small and specific instance, refusing.

The refusal had a shape. The shape was love.

She was not going to say it. She was not going to think it. She was going to need a chemist, and the chemist she could get to in the next hour was Adrian, and the question of whether she could trust Adrian was a question she would have to ask a version of herself who had slept.

She opened her comm. She typed a single line.

Need your chemistry eye on something. Come when you can.

She pressed send.

The reply came in sixteen seconds.

On my way.

Six

He came with his own slate.

Nia opened the door to find Adrian standing in the corridor, a soft leather case tucked under one arm. The junior officer was already retreating three doors down the hall to give them distance. Adrian looked at the junior officer once and then at Nia. He did not comment on the distance.

He came inside. He set the case on the table by the door, took off his coat, and hung it on the hook where he had hung it last night.

"I didn't want to come on the embassy terminal," he said.

"Mm," Nia said.

"This one's mine. Off-service. Same certificates."

"All right."

He followed her to the small desk in the alcove and pulled up a second chair. She was already back at the terminal, the olfactory simulator still on the desk beside her, the phones hooked over the slate. She gestured at the chair and he sat. He opened his case. His slate was older than the embassy's, an academic model from six or seven years back, with the kind of keyboard chemists still preferred for writing formulas. He turned it on.

"What have you got," he said.

She showed him.

She showed him her time-stamp of the poison's arrival. She showed him the color map with the southwest upper volume highlighted. She showed him the seven features she had matched to the Fifth Current aggression register, and the ten library papers she had traced them to. She showed him the thirteen features she could not match to anything.

She did not show him Halpern-Ødegård's report. She did not show him the paragraph about the forger reading the library copy. She wanted to hear him describe what he was seeing before she let him see what she had already concluded.

He read in the particular way he had always read: leaning slightly forward, left hand curled around his jaw, right hand on the controls. It had been one of the things she had found attractive at twenty-four and unendurable at twenty-six. At thirty-one she was watching for it again, in order to decide whether she still knew him.

He took nine minutes. Nia timed it.

When he sat back he did not look at her first. He looked at the ceiling. He breathed out.

"The thirteen features are not Thren," he said.

"I know."

"They're synthetic."

"I thought so."

"They're synthesized by a method called Kallmann-Iwasaki enrichment."

Nia, who did not know the method, wrote the name in her notes.

"What is that," she said.

"It's a way of stabilizing a chemical signature so that it propagates through a specific atmospheric medium without degrading. Developed about twelve years ago for industrial flavoring applications. You want a given scent to survive a warm moist transit without the upper notes dropping off. Food-service, initially. Then perfumery. Then, a few years ago, it got picked up by a couple of research labs working on suspension-adjacent chemistry."

"Suspension-adjacent."

"The suspension is a warm moist medium."

"Yes."

"Kallmann-Iwasaki is a way to make a chemical signature survive a warm moist medium with the upper notes intact."

"Yes."

"Whoever built this thing wanted it to arrive in the suspension looking exactly the way they had designed it to look."

She sat with this for a moment. She did not write it down.

"Would I have known this method," she said.

"No."

"You would have."

"Yes."

"Because it's your field."

"Because it's my field."

He said it without inflection, the way he had said the previous three lines. It was the kind of clarity she had always liked in him, when he was working. She chose to register it as professional.

"Which labs," she said.

"Which labs use Kallmann-Iwasaki for suspension-adjacent work, or which labs could have built this?"

"Which labs could have built this."

He reached for her notes. She let him have them. He wrote a list.

Halden-Voss Industrial Flavors. Cascade Scent Technologies. Thirdwater Research. Argent Molecular. A fifth lab whose name she could not immediately read, because his handwriting had always been worse than his typing.

"Five," he said.

"Five."

"Three are industrial flavoring houses with no reason to be building anything that could pass as Thren speech. Two are research labs. One of those two is in your field."

"Which."

"Thirdwater."

Nia wrote it down twice. Once under the list, once at the top of a fresh line in her private notes.

"What do you know about Thirdwater," she said.

"Small. Privately held. Publishes in the open literature about once a year. The paper eight months ago, the one I mentioned to you in the garden. Do you remember."

"No."

"I must not have, then. Suspension-propagation study. Came out in the open Thren chemistry quarterly. I thought it was a good paper."

"Did you."

"It was a careful paper. They knew what they were doing."

"Who is they."

"I don't remember the authors. I'll pull it up at the wing."

Nia looked at him. He was sitting back in the chair now, both hands at his sides, his face arranged in the careful non-expression that she had been noticing was his face for her since she had come home last night. It was not an unhelpful face. It was the face of a man doing his best to be the ally she needed him to be, and to hold, separately and in a part of himself he was not letting her see, something he had not been able to let her see.

She did not ask him what the something was.

She had her list.

She had, in fact, more than a list. She had a specific method, a specific medium-compatibility profile, and a specific narrow field of labs with the capability. She had an ask she could now send to her old thesis advisor, who ran the Thren chemical communication seminar at the Concordance Academy and would know the narrow field by name. She had the shape of an afternoon's work ahead of her that was, for the first time since yesterday, work she could do.

She had also, she noticed, been careful not to say the name Vorathan since he had walked in.

"Thank you," she said.

"Nee."

"I mean it. Thank you."

"You're not going to tell me about the Thren, are you."

"No."

"Okay."

He stood. He did not come to the couch this time. He stayed by the desk. He put one hand on the back of her chair and let it rest there for about two seconds. Then he removed it and picked up his case.

"Call if you need anything else from me," he said.

"I will."

"Get some sleep, Nee."

"I will."

He did not say she was lying. He went to the door, opened it, closed it behind him. She listened for his steps, which were uneven in the first four paces in a way that was not the way his steps usually were, and then evened out by the time he reached the junction. She listened to the junior officer's steps adjusting again.

She sat at the desk for a full minute after they were gone.

Then she looked at the list of five labs.

Thirdwater Research. She had seen the name before. A recruiter had come to the Academy in her second year of doctoral work. A private-sector fellowship, three times the Concordance stipend, full chemistry-lab access, relocation to a compound she had not heard of in the Outer Belt. She had said no politely. She had not, until now, thought of it again.

She pulled up the open Thren chemistry quarterly archive.

She found the paper from eight months ago.

She began to read.

Seven

The paper was, when read in the right order, a confession.

Nia did not read it in that order at first. She read it the way a linguist reads a paper outside her field: abstract, introduction, methods, results, discussion, conclusion, back to abstract. She took twenty minutes on the abstract and came up with nothing that alarmed her. The paper described a specific application of Kallmann-Iwasaki enrichment to suspension-adjacent chemical signatures. It characterized, in dry professional prose, a method for stabilizing a complex chemical signal so it could survive a warm moist transit without degradation. The application frame was environmental. The authors argued the method had value for monitoring trace atmospheric pollutants in closed biospheres, particularly in long-rotation research stations where chemical signal integrity mattered for instrument calibration.

It was, Nia thought, a reasonable cover.

She went back to the introduction and read more slowly.

The introduction cited twelve prior papers on Kallmann-Iwasaki. It cited six papers on Thren chemistry. It cited two papers on the chemistry of ceremonial-space atmospheric monitoring, which was a niche Nia had not known existed. She wrote the niche down in her notes as a thing to investigate. The introduction did not describe the authors' prior work. Most papers in a narrow field opened by situating the authors' own prior contribution. This one skipped that move. Nia flagged it.

She read the methods section.

The methods were where the paper became specific. The authors described a synthesis protocol that began with a standard Kallmann-Iwasaki base and added thirteen modifying features in a particular sequence. They did not, in the methods proper, say what the thirteen features were for. They described the sequence. They described the reagents. They described the temperature curves and the catalyst ratios. They described the method of introducing the modified signal into a test volume. They described the test volume's dimensions.

Nia read the dimensions twice.

The test volume was eight meters by eight meters by four meters high.

She did not, off the top of her head, know the dimensions of the Sepharu audience chamber. She had seen the numbers on the orientation slides on day one. She had not memorized them. She had assumed she would never need to.

She opened the embassy's Sepharu audience chamber specifications, which were in the general-access section of the delegation briefing materials.

The audience chamber was eight meters by eight meters by four meters high.

She wrote the correspondence down. She did not underline it. She moved on.

The results section described what the modified signal looked like after introduction into the test volume. The authors had generated a panel of seven analogue signatures based on the published Thren chemical literature. They had introduced each into the test volume in turn. They had measured the dispersal pattern, the persistence, and the recognition signal to trained human observers watching remotely. The paper included, in its figures, color maps of the seven signatures unfurling through the test volume in slow branching strokes.

The figures were not labeled with Thren source material. Nia did not need the labels. She recognized the first signature inside a second of opening the figure. It was a branching pattern from one of the most cited references in the public Thren chemistry literature, the kind of feature any second-year graduate student in her field could name. She had memorized it herself, years ago, for a comprehensive exam. The second figure was the same. The third was the same.

The seven signatures matched the seven most cited features of the Fifth Current aggression register.

The paper was a blueprint.

It was not presented as a blueprint. It was presented as a careful methodology study on Kallmann-Iwasaki suspension-adjacent chemistry, whose application frame happened to require the generation of Thren-analogue test signals in a chamber of standard embassy dimensions. If anyone had asked the authors, on the day of publication, whether their paper was the design document for a Thren-impersonating poison that would pass at a first reading and could be released into a real embassy chamber with a calibrated payload, they would have said no with professional clarity. The paper would have supported that answer. The paper, Nia suspected, had been written to support that answer.

She went to the author list.

There were four authors.

Three of them were names Nia did not know, which she took as the normal condition of a chemistry paper she had not been reading as a chemist.

The fourth name was Dr. Yuji Park.

She had seen the name before. She had seen it on the cover of a paper Adrian had co-authored three years before, a study of chemical signal degradation at low-pressure boundaries, where Park had been second author to Adrian's first. She had seen the name again about eight months ago, on a conference program from a Concordance chemistry symposium Adrian had attended in the Outer Belt. She had seen the name a third time, on the masthead of a small journal Adrian sometimes guest-edited, of which Park was an associate.

She sat back from the slate.

Adrian had told her, that afternoon, that he did not remember the authors of the Thirdwater paper.

He would remember Yuji Park.

She did not think he had forgotten. She thought he had said he had forgotten, which was not the same thing. It was one of the tells she had been refusing to name since last night.

She did not name it now, either.

She closed the paper. She opened the Concordance publication database. She typed Adrian's name.

The database returned forty-seven papers across twelve years of career. She filtered to the last five years. The database returned nineteen.

She opened the first one that was not hers.

It was a 2186 paper on the chemistry of trace contamination in long-rotation life support, with three co-authors. None was Park. The work was unrelated to her question. She tagged it for later reading and moved on.

She opened the second.

Park was second author.

She opened the third. Park was an acknowledged technical reviewer.

She tagged both.

Her comm chirped.

She did not look. She was reading.

It chirped again, two beats later.

She looked. Adrian. Checking on her. Telling her to get some sleep.

She did not reply.

She turned back to the database.

Eight

Dhillon called at 03:46 local.

Nia had not slept. She had been reading Adrian's papers in the order they had been published. She had been tagging the ones with Park as co-author or technical reviewer or acknowledged collaborator, and the count was at four out of seven, which was statistically more than she would have expected from a chemist who had supposedly forgotten Park's name. She picked up the call on the third chirp.

"Doctor."

"Dhillon."

"I wanted you to hear it from me. The Chair has scheduled a vote on the preliminary finding for the Parliament's afternoon session. Local time fifteen hundred. They will vote to adopt the Halpern-Ødegård report as the working determination."

"That's eleven hours."

"Eleven by clock. Closer to seven by what you can do with them."

"You are calling me at four in the morning to tell me this."

"I am calling you at four in the morning so that you have eleven hours instead of nine."

She was quiet.

"I am not going to be in a position to slow this down inside the service," Dhillon said. "I want you to understand that."

"I understand."

"If you have something, give it to me by fourteen hundred. I will put it in front of the Chair if I can."

"All right."

"Nia."

"Yes."

"Get it to me by fourteen hundred."

He ended the call.

She set the slate on the desk. She sat with her hands in her lap. The simulated sky above her had been on the deep cold dark of the sleep cycle for nine hours. It would shift to dawn in another forty minutes. She would have light to think by then. She did not think she needed it.

What she had: a blueprint paper that was, on a careful reading, the exact technology used to kill Vance. A pattern of citations and co-authorships placing Adrian inside the network that produced the paper. A specific named witness she could not yet name aloud, because he was a friend.

What she did not have: independent corroboration from anyone outside the network. Without that, the blueprint was a published study, the citations were academic, and the named witness was a personal grievance dressed up as evidence. The Parliament would adopt the report at fifteen hundred and the Halpern-Ødegård determination would become the public record. She could spend the next year of her life chipping at that record. She would not unmake it before the Thren had folded any further into withdrawn hearing than they had already folded.

She needed a Thren reading. She needed it from a Thren who would say in chemistry what no Thren in the audience chamber was willing to say in speech.

She thought of Vorathan.

She had not spoken to him. He had not spoken to her. He had presented himself across a glass partition for five seconds in ceremonial collars and had cycled four signatures on the underside of a limb. She had returned a hand-gesture. They had agreed to nothing, because they had said nothing. He could not come to her quarters. She could not go to him. The civil service was watching her comm and her terminal and her door and the corridor and the garden access points.

The garden access points.

The garden was monitored.

It was monitored because every closed biosphere on Sepharu was monitored, and the Concordance gardens were closed biospheres. The monitoring system tracked atmospheric composition, humidity, and trace chemical signal anomalies. The last of these was there because the embassy botanists had wanted to know if any of their Terran grass cultivars were releasing volatiles that did not belong in a Sepharu environment. The monitoring was indiscriminate. The system did not know Thren chemical speech from a botanical anomaly. It logged both at the same priority.

Nia opened the embassy environmental monitoring portal.

She had general-access read permission from her junior linguist credentials.

She filtered to the garden.

She filtered to the past forty-eight hours.

She filtered to anomalies tagged as unidentified or atmospheric, anything the system did not have a category for.

The portal returned eleven entries.

Eight were dawn fungal blooms. Two were minor humidity irregularities. The eleventh was a chemical signature recorded yesterday at 07:18 local, six minutes after Vorathan had walked away from the glass partition.

Nia opened it.

The signature was small. The system had logged it as unidentified atmospheric trace, low priority. The system had not flagged it as Thren because the system was not tuned to read Thren chemical speech. It had recorded what it recorded as raw chemical composition data.

Nia loaded the data into her chemistry tools.

She read it.

It was a fingerprint.

It was a structural signature, complete with branching vectors, dispersal pattern, and a small annotated marker at the upper-left corner that she did not at first recognize. The fingerprint matched the poison from the chamber. Not approximately. Exactly. Vorathan had read the poison's chemistry while standing in the alcove. He had held the structure in memory for twenty hours. He had reproduced it at the molecular level and released it in the garden where the embassy's own monitoring system would record it for her to find.

She sat with this for a moment.

Then she looked at the marker.

The marker was a citation. Vorathan had tagged the signature with a chemical reference to a published paper.

The identifier was rendered in Concordance journal-citation format, which a Thren scholar would have learned only by reading human chemistry literature.

She pulled up the citation.

It was a Thren chemistry paper from the open quarterly. It was one of the six Thren chemistry papers cited in the Thirdwater blueprint.

She sat back.

Vorathan had read the Thirdwater paper.

He had read it. He had told her, in a chemical signature in a garden at 07:18 local, that he understood what it was, and that the poison's chemistry matched it.

She did not yet know how a Thren scholar of the Fourth Current had acquired access to a Concordance chemistry quarterly. She would, eventually, ask. She did not need to ask now.

She had her corroboration.

She had it twelve hours before fifteen hundred.

She closed the portal.

She opened a fresh document.

She began to write a brief.

Nine

By thirteen hundred she had rewritten the brief four times.

The first version had been a full academic treatment: methodology, evidence, citations, conclusion. Eighteen pages. It had read, she realized on the second pass, like a thesis defense against a committee that was not in the room. She cut it.

The second version had been a prosecution brief: the blueprint, the methods match, the dimensions correspondence, Vorathan's independent chemical corroboration, a timeline. Twelve pages. It had read, she realized on the third pass, like a brief that named Adrian without ever mentioning him. She cut that too.

The fourth version, which was the one she sent, was four pages.

It argued three things. One: the chemical analysis used to attribute the poison to the Fifth Current had relied on the seven features most commonly cited in the public literature, and had omitted the thirteen features for which no Thren analogue existed. Two: a published chemistry paper eight months old from Thirdwater Research documented the capability to produce exactly this chemistry in a test volume of the exact dimensions of the Sepharu audience chamber. Three: an independent Thren scholar, whose identity she was declining to name, had produced a molecular fingerprint of the poison and tagged it with a citation corroborating both of the above.

She attached the supporting files. She requested a postponement of the fifteen-hundred vote on those grounds.

She signed it Dr. Iyana Okafor-Reyes, Principal Linguist, Sepharu Delegation, and sent it to Dhillon at 13:42.

The reply came in two minutes. Come to my office.

The junior officer at her door was not the one who had been there overnight. He had been replaced once at 06:00 and once at 12:00, both times by another junior officer of the same pay grade and similar posture. The current one was a woman Nia had not seen before. She looked at Nia with neither hostility nor warmth, which was the expression a service member wore when she had been briefed only to the level of the assignment and had decided not to ask for more.

Nia said she was going to Dhillon's office.

The officer said she was going to walk Nia there.

They walked.

The compound at thirteen forty-five was in the quiet of a workday afternoon. The corridors were not empty. They were full in the particular way they were full when people were moving without meeting each other's eyes. Nia had been in this kind of compound quiet before. It was the quiet of a service waiting for a vote that had already been decided and was pretending not to know it. The silence was different from the silence after Vance had died. The silence after Vance had been grief. This was administration.

She passed Adaeze Okonkwo at the junction of the residential and civil service wings. Adaeze looked up, saw Nia, and did not look away. She held Nia's eyes for about two seconds, and in those two seconds she performed the small service-internal gesture that meant, approximately: I see you, I cannot help you, I hope it works.

Nia nodded once.

Adaeze looked down.

Dhillon's outer door was open when they arrived.

Dhillon was alone. There was no legal counsel this time, and no man in charcoal, and no dataslate waiting to be thumbed. There was only Dhillon, sitting at the round table, a printed copy of Nia's brief in front of him and a pen in his hand. He had underlined things. He had underlined a lot of things.

The junior officer paused at the doorway.

"Thank you," Dhillon said. He did not dismiss her. He gave her a chair in the anteroom and closed the inner door.

Nia sat.

"Four pages," Dhillon said.

"Four pages."

"You could have given me thirty."

"Thirty wouldn't fit in the Chair's remaining hour."

"No."

He looked at the brief. He did not look at her. He was reading, again, one of the underlined passages, probably the one about the Thirdwater paper's test volume dimensions, which was the single paragraph that did the most work in the shortest space.

"The Thren source," he said.

"I'm not going to name the source."

"I am not asking you to."

"All right."

"But I need to understand what I am walking into the Chair's office with. The Chair will ask me how confident I am in the corroboration, and I need to be able to answer without lying. I cannot do that if I do not know whether your Thren source is a minor scholar, a senior political figure, or a dead man."

"Scholar."

"Minor or senior."

"Minor."

"Current."

"I am not going to name the Current."

"Nia."

"Dhillon."

"The Fourth."

"I am not going to name the Current."

"All right."

He went back to the brief. He underlined one more thing, which she could not read upside-down. He set the pen down.

"Doctor," he said. "I want to ask you something I am not going to put in the record."

"Yes."

"Your brief does not name a suspect."

"No."

"The chemistry trail you describe leads to a human actor with specialized knowledge of Thren chemical communication. That actor, whoever they are, is a person you know the name of."

"Yes."

"And are not going to tell me."

"Not today."

"All right."

He looked at her for a long moment.

"When you are ready to share the name," he said, "come to me first. Not the service. Not the Chair. Me."

"All right."

"Good."

He picked up the brief and the pen and stood.

"I am going to the Chair now," he said. "I will be back in an hour, or I will not. If you do not hear from me by sixteen hundred, it did not work."

"All right."

"Go back to your quarters, Doctor."

She stood.

He met her eye. He did not smile. He did, for a fraction of a second that would not have been visible to anyone who had not been reading faces for a living for ten years, look at her the way a senior diplomat looks at a junior one he has decided to trust.

She nodded.

She left the office.

The junior officer was in the anteroom chair. She stood when Nia came out. They walked back through the compound in the same quiet, and at the junction Adaeze was not there. They reached Nia's door. The officer stopped at the correct distance. Nia went inside.

She sat down at the desk. She did not open the terminal. She did not turn on the slate.

She looked at the simulated sky, which was on the particular late-afternoon cycle the compound ran between thirteen and seventeen hundred, a soft gold the embassy designers had calibrated to suggest the warmth of a weekend.

She waited.

Ten

She had told herself she would not watch the clock.

She did not need to watch it. The compound had its own time, and she had spent enough hours in it to know what color the light was at fifteen hundred, at fifteen thirty, at sixteen hundred. The simulated sky did her waiting for her. She sat at the desk with her hands in her lap. Then she sat on the couch with her hands in her lap. Then she made tea she did not drink. Through all of it the sky moved from the warm gold of weekend afternoon toward the thinning orange that meant the evening cycle was about to begin.

Sixteen hundred came. No message.

She waited for Dhillon to be wrong. He had said sixteen hundred. He had also been careful enough to tell her that sixteen hundred was the deadline, not the guarantee. She sat with that for four more minutes. At sixteen oh four the thin orange began to deepen, which was the compound's marker for the evening cycle beginning in earnest.

She understood.

Her comm chirped at sixteen fourteen.

The message was from Dhillon. The Parliament had adopted the Halpern-Ødegård report as the working determination. Her brief had been entered into the record. The Chair had asked for her name to be noted. She had been thanked for her service.

She read it twice.

She closed the comm.

She sat for a long moment with her hands in her lap, looking at the ceiling panel, which was already shifting toward the deeper dusk of the full evening cycle. She did not feel much of anything. She thought, distantly, that she should feel something, and then she thought that she would probably feel it later, and then she thought that her training had taught her to register the felt thing and the unfelt thing as two different kinds of data, and then she stopped thinking.

She stood up.

The small bathroom off her quarters had a shower she had been ignoring for thirty-two hours. She turned the water on and let it run while she took off her clothes. She stepped in. The water was warm. She did not lather or scrub. She stood under the water with her eyes closed, and let it land on her shoulders, her back, the top of her head. She breathed. The water tasted of the compound's recycling system, which was a taste she had learned to ignore on day three. She let it be in her mouth now. She did not spit it out. It was water.

She stayed under the shower for twenty minutes.

When she stepped out, her skin was pink and her fingertips were wrinkled, and the tile of the bathroom floor was warm through the pads of her feet. She wrapped a towel around herself. She did not look in the mirror. She did not need to. She was not a person who needed to see her own face at sixteen forty in the evening cycle of the day after she had failed to stop a Parliament vote.

She went to the galley alcove.

There was a meal pack in the cooling drawer. She did not remember when she had bought it. She heated it. It was a spiced rice dish with cultivated protein and a sauce she had always suspected of being mostly paprika. She ate half of it standing at the counter. She put the other half back in the drawer. She drank two glasses of water.

She went to the bed.

She had not slept in the bed since the first night. She had slept, if one could call what she had done sleep, on the couch. The bed was still made from the orientation housekeeping on day one. She pulled back the covers. She lay down.

The simulated sky above the bed was calibrated on a different cycle than the one in the main room. It was already on the sleep cycle, the deep cold dark the embassy designers had chosen to approximate Earth winter night. She watched it for a long moment. She closed her eyes.

Her body had been waiting for permission.

It took it.

She slept.

Eleven

She slept for nine hours.

The dawn cycle was already on when she opened her eyes, which meant the compound had moved into its Sepharu-morning register some time while she had been unconscious. She lay in the bed for a minute without moving, taking inventory. Her shoulders and back were sore. Her hands were sore in a way that surprised her until she remembered she had spent most of the previous afternoon holding a pen she had not needed to hold. The inside of her mouth tasted of last night's water. Her chest was, for the first time in three days, not tight.

She sat up.

She drank water. She put on a robe. She made coffee. She drank the coffee standing at the counter, because it felt good to be upright and not exhausted.

She checked her comm.

Three messages. The first was from Dhillon, sent at 22:14 local. It was one sentence: I am sorry, and I am not done. She read it twice and did not reply.

The second was from Ilsia Moreau, the embassy's embedded journalist, sent at 07:40. It was a long paragraph. It said Ilsia had been tracking the Parliament proceedings. She had read the transcript of the Chair's remarks. She had noted Nia's name in the record. She would welcome a conversation at any time of Nia's choosing, on or off the record. Nia read it twice and did not reply.

The third message was from Adrian. It said he was thinking about her. It said he was available. Nia did not read it twice.

She sat at the desk.

She opened the embassy monitoring portal and pulled up Vorathan's garden signature from yesterday. She read it again even though she didn't need to. She was reading it for a different reason now. Yesterday she had read it for what it told her about the poison. Today she was reading it for what it told her about Vorathan.

He had released a molecular fingerprint of the poison in the garden. He had tagged it with a citation to a Thirdwater-cited paper. He had done this at personal cost, from a Current that did not want its members associated with the Concordance investigation, at a time when the Thren had folded into the deepest ritual silence available to them. He had done it for Nia, because he had trusted that Nia would find it.

He had also done it, she understood now, because he wanted her to speak back.

She could not go to the garden. The civil service was watching her comm, her terminal, her door, and the garden access points. She was confined to her quarters. The confinement was informal, framed as welfare, enforceable only through embarrassment and inconvenience. It was not going to be lifted. It was going to be tightened the moment she tried to circumvent it.

Unless she asked to go.

The Concordance embassy on Sepharu had a standing protocol for scholarly field work, which permitted junior delegates to conduct short supervised visits to the compound's enclosed biosphere for professional purposes, provided the purpose was documented and the request was approved by the acting head of delegation. Nia had read the protocol on day two, as part of her orientation, and had filed the existence of it away as one of the small administrative facts a scholar in her field noticed automatically.

She opened the request form.

What she needed was a professional reason to stand in the garden for thirty minutes.

What she had was the truth. She did not want to use the truth.

She thought about this for a while. Then she thought about what she would have done if she had been a different kind of person, one who had not been writing a request to a Concordance senior diplomat whose ability to read her intention she had spent three days confirming. The answer was: a different kind of person would have lied. Nia was not going to lie to Dhillon. She was also not going to say, in a formal request, that she was going to the garden to leave a chemical message for a Thren scholar.

She wrote: Chemical baseline survey of the compound biosphere for ongoing Thren-human comparative atmospheric study. Access requested for thirty minutes of quiet standing observation, no equipment, no samples. Scholarly use only.

She reread it. It was true. It was also not the whole truth, but none of it was false. She sent it.

The terminal pinged four minutes later.

Request approved. Escort to be provided at your door at ten thirty.

She looked at the time. 09:47.

She had forty-three minutes.

She closed the terminal. She went to the small closet in the corner of the room, pulled down the one suitcase she had brought from Earth, and opened it. Inside, wrapped in a linen cloth that had been her mother's, was a small case of glass vials she had carried through customs on three planets. Each vial held a single synthesized chemical signature, keyed in her private notation to a phrase, stable for three years, legal for scholarly transport under the Concordance's cross-species research protocols. She had brought them because she had thought she might need to talk.

She opened the case.

She chose two vials.

The first was keyed to the phrase the Thren used when the available channels for a question had closed.

The second was keyed to the name of the mourning.

Twelve

The escort came at ten thirty.

Nia opened the door to the same junior officer who had walked her back from Dhillon's office the day before, wearing the same neutral expression, holding the same posture. Nia had her coat on. The vials were in the inside breast pocket, padded by the linen cloth that had been her mother's. She had practiced the gesture, while she was waiting, of reaching for them with her right hand and uncapping each with her thumb in a single fluid motion. She had practiced it twice without dropping anything, and three times after that with her eyes closed.

"Doctor," the officer said.

"Yes."

"Garden access for thirty minutes. Acting head of delegation has signed it. I will accompany you to the garden, remain inside the threshold, and accompany you back. You are not to bring instruments or take samples."

"I understand."

"Please."

She went where the officer turned her.

The corridor to the garden had a particular humidity that the rest of the compound did not have, because the garden was a closed biosphere and the sealing system equalized atmospheric water content along the approach so the visitor would not notice the moisture step. Nia noticed the step. She had been trained to notice atmospheric transitions in the years before she had ever stood in the suspension. She was noticing one now.

The corridor opened into the airlock, which was a small chamber with two doors that did not open at the same time. The officer cycled the inner door. The outer door opened onto the garden.

Nia walked in.

The garden was twenty meters across at its widest. The lawn was kept Terran grass cultivated under a low sun lamp the embassy designers had calibrated to feel approximately like a late afternoon in Northern California, an aesthetic decision the embassy botanists had endorsed and the rest of the staff had accepted without complaint. There was a path of pale gravel that ran the length of the garden along the long axis. There were three benches at intervals. There was, at the far end, the low glass partition Nia had stood beside two days earlier, when a Thren scholar she did not yet know the name of had cycled four signatures on the underside of a limb and walked away.

She walked to the bench nearest the partition.

She did not sit on it.

She turned, slowly, in the place where she had stood before, and let her eye move over the volume of the garden. The air was warm. The light was warm. The grass smelled, when the system's circulating fans moved past, of cut Earth grass under Earth sun, which was a smell she had not expected to feel as strongly as she felt it.

She had three minutes to compose herself before the officer would begin to wonder why she was not standing still.

She composed herself.

She turned her back to the officer, who was at the threshold, and put her right hand into the inside breast pocket of her coat. She uncapped the first vial with her thumb. She held it in her palm at her side, low, and let the signature it carried drift into the volume of the garden through the gap between her thumb and her forefinger.

The signature was small. The garden's air-circulation system would carry it slowly along the long axis of the lawn, against the glass partition, where it would settle into the volume Vorathan had used for his own release. The system would log it as an atmospheric anomaly, low priority. By the time the system flagged it, the signature would have settled into the air at the partition. If Vorathan was watching for a reply, he would read it the way he had spoken: in the air. If he was not watching, the signature would degrade in seventy-two hours and be carried out by the circulation system.

The first vial took about ninety seconds to empty.

She moved it from her right hand to her left. She put the second vial in her right hand. She released it the same way.

The second signature joined the first in the volume above the bench, and the two of them drifted, very slowly, in the warm light of the garden.

She closed her eyes for a moment.

She listened.

Not to anything human or Thren. To the air-handling system's quiet hum, to the distant tick of the lamp's fixture as it adjusted, to her own breath.

She had spoken.

She turned and walked back along the gravel path. She did not look at the officer until she reached the threshold. The officer met her eye and nodded once. Nia nodded back. The airlock cycled.

The walk through the corridor was the opposite of her walk in. The humidity stepped down. The compound's quieter atmosphere replaced the garden's. Nia counted her breaths for the first thirty seconds and then stopped. She thought about Vance, briefly, and then she stopped that too. She had work waiting for her in her quarters and very little time in which to do it. If Vorathan was reading the garden at any reasonable cadence, she should expect a reply by the end of the local day.

The officer brought her to her door.

The officer did not go inside. Instead, she turned and walked back down the corridor. Nia heard her steps fade to the junction.

She went into her quarters.

She took off her coat.

She hung it on the hook.

She sat down at the desk, opened the embassy environmental monitoring portal, filtered to the garden, and set a real-time alert on any new unidentified atmospheric trace.

She waited.

Thirteen

By thirteen hundred she had read everything the Concordance library had on the Thren mourning rite, which was less than she had hoped and more than she had known existed.

The public-facing literature treated the rite as a category. It was named in three places in the standard ethnographic surveys: as a Thren grief practice (correct, incomplete), as a chemical-vocal-pigment ceremony reserved for family-level standing (correct, important), and as a forensic compulsion at the deepest register of Thren chemical communication (correct, the part nobody had wanted to name). The forensic register was mentioned in a single footnote in a single Concordance ethnographic paper from twelve years ago. The footnote cited a Thren oral source the author had not been allowed to name. Nia read the footnote twice. She read the citations. She read the citations of the citations. She found nothing more.

What was not in the public literature was the actual sequence of the rite. The phrasing. The chemical phrases. The ritual gestures. The standing required of the speaker. The standing required of the witnesses. Everything that would let a person actually perform the mourning was held by Thren scholars, and the Thren did not publish on it.

She closed the library.

She sat for a moment.

She had first encountered the rite in the fourth year of her doctoral work, in a seminar Professor Obi-Halloran had taught on Thren chemical ethics. The seminar had been attended by seven students. The rite had been discussed in one session. Professor Obi-Halloran had called it the deepest form Thren chemistry had produced, and had followed that, in her precise and exhausted way, by saying she hoped none of them would ever see it performed. Nia had written the statement down. She had not understood, at twenty-five, why the hope had been phrased as a wish.

She understood now.

In the recorded history of the Seven Currents, the mourning rite had been performed four times the Thren acknowledged publicly, and probably twice more in internal Current records the Concordance had never been shown. Nia knew the four. She had written a seminar paper on them, which was the only paper she had ever written that had received no comments from Professor Obi-Halloran. The professor had been one of the two humans ever granted observer standing in the Seventh Current, and she had taken a silence on the rite as a condition of that standing that she had never broken.

The first recorded performance had been two hundred and seventy Thren years before contact, inside the First Current, at a ceremony of succession. A claimant to the First-Speaker's standing had been revealed, by the rite's compulsion, to be a chemical impostor whose lineage did not carry the seven inherited signatures of the Current.

The rite had exposed the claimant without words. The Current had acted on that exposure. The claimant had been, in Nia's notation, set down, which was a Thren term that permitted some variation in its execution.

The second had been performed a hundred and thirty years later, inside the Third Current, to investigate the poisoning of a scholar whose work had been inconvenient to the Current's elders. The rite had not exposed a member of the Third Current. It had exposed one of the elders.

The third had been performed by a cross-Current council sixty years before contact, after a treaty between the Second and Sixth Currents had been broken by a single act of sabotage no Current was willing to claim. The rite had compelled response across both Currents. The saboteur had been a speaker the council had trusted. He had been set down, the term kept careful.

The fourth had been performed inside the Sixth Current in the years since contact. It had been described in the public literature only as a purification. The thing being purified had not been named.

Four performances across two hundred and seventy years. Each one forensic. Each one expensive to the performer, who absorbed the compulsion the rite cast. Two of the four performers had survived. The other two had not. The survivors had been performing inside a Current, for that Current, with the Current's elders standing beside them. The two who had not survived had been performing across Currents, against a target the Current had not expected the rite to find.

Nia had a target no Current was expecting.

She had been wrong about what she had been asking Vorathan to do.

She had assumed Vorathan would respond with information she could act on. She had assumed the mourning was an idea she could carry forward in her own head, with him as a consultant on Thren practice. She understood, sitting in the silent quarters at thirteen oh six in the afternoon, that she had asked him to teach her something only Thren scholars knew. To tell her would be to break the same kind of silence the Thren had folded into around her.

She did not unsend the message. She could not have, and she would not have if she could.

She made tea. She drank it. She did not eat.

She rechecked the alert at thirteen forty-five. Nothing. She rechecked it at fourteen thirty. Nothing. She rechecked it at fifteen fifteen. Nothing.

At sixteen forty-two the alert pinged.

She opened the portal.

The new signature was in the garden, recorded six minutes earlier, tagged as unidentified atmospheric trace, low priority. The system had logged it as a single anomaly, which meant the system was reading it as one event. Nia knew, before she opened it, that it was not one event. Vorathan would not have come to the partition to release one phrase. He would have come to release as many as he could fit in the window he had.

She opened the data.

It was four signatures.

She loaded them in sequence.

The first was the Thren acknowledgment. He had read what she had released. He had heard her ask the question.

The second was the mourning name, repeated back to her in his register. It was not a denial. It was a confirmation that he had understood which mourning she meant, and that there was only one mourning that bore that name.

The third was longer. It was a phrase she had to read twice, look up in her own notation, and then read again. It rendered, approximately, as: the rite is held by the speakers, the speakers are seven, six may hear you, one will refuse. The grammar carried a specific Thren register her notation had not been built to translate fully, but she had enough. Six of the Seven Currents could be approached for permission. The Fifth Current would refuse her, which made sense, because the Fifth Current was the Current the Halpern-Ødegård report had named.

The fourth signature was the longest, and the one she sat with the longest after reading.

It rendered, approximately, as: the mourning is finished by the body that begins it.

She read the fourth signature three times. She did not need to look it up. The Thren grammar of finished by the body that begins it was as clear as anything in the language. The performer of the rite was the one the rite consumed.

She sat back.

She had asked. He had answered.

The answer was that she could perform the mourning. Six Currents could be approached for permission. The Fifth would refuse her. The rite would cost her her body in some way she did not yet understand. He had not, in four signatures, been willing to specify.

She had her path.

She had not been promised it would not cost her her life.

She thought about this for a long time. She did not make a list. She did not draft a request. She did not write a brief. She sat at the desk with her hands flat on the surface and she thought.

When she stood up it was eighteen oh four in the early evening cycle.

She had decided.

She opened a fresh request form to Dhillon. She wrote: I need to speak with the senior Thren hosts. Not through the formal channel. Privately. Today.

She sent it.

Fourteen

She had, when she closed the message to Dhillon, seventeen minutes before he would reply.

She did not intend to spend them at the terminal. She had intended to stand, drink water, and wait in a chair. She did not do those things. She opened the library again. She opened the expanded entry on the Sixth Current purification.

The expanded entry had not come up in her first search. Her credentials had not reached it then. They reached it now. She understood, from the note at the top of the file, that the Sixth Current had made the record available to her because she had asked, publicly, for the name of the mourning. It had not been flagged to her. It was there because she had, in the view of the Current that had maintained the record, earned standing.

She did not stop to consider what that standing was. She opened the record.

The record was titled, in Sixth Current formal notation, The Fourth Purification. The date was given in two registers: the Thren imperial calendar, which placed it in the fourteenth year of the post-contact measure, and the

Concordance standard calendar, which placed it in the late winter of the year before Nia had begun her doctoral work.

She had been at the Academy that year. She had been twenty-one. She had not heard of the event at the time. She now understood that as a Sixth Current choice.

The record opened with a paragraph of context.

"In the eleventh month of the fourteenth year, a chemical phrase native to the Sixth Current's grief-register was recovered from the shared inter-Current library, and was determined on examination to have been modified. The modification altered the grief-phrase into a form that, when released in the presence of a Fifth Current listener, read as ritual challenge. The modification was subtle. It had been in the library for an estimated four Thren years before its recovery."

Nia paused on four Thren years. Seven of her own. The falsified phrase had been circulating in the Thren record for nearly seven years before anyone had noticed it.

"On the twenty-third day of the eleventh month, a Fifth Current delegation attended a consultation of the Sixth. They heard the phrase as it had been falsified, and they responded with the contempt the falsified phrase required. The Sixth Current delegation, not recognizing that its own phrase had been altered, received the response as contempt offered without cause. The consultation broke. Two speakers of the Sixth Current, in the hours that followed, died of a cascade failure of their signature-regulation that the Current at the time attributed to the shock of the broken consultation."

Nia read the paragraph twice. The manner of the two deaths was a manner she had read about once in graduate school, in a paper she no longer remembered the author of: the body unable to contain its own signature, flooding its own regulators, collapsing from within. Not poisoning. Self-dissolution.

"The Current convened an internal investigation. The investigation located the falsification in the library record within the following week. It did not locate the authoring speaker. The falsified phrase was quarantined in the library and flagged. It could not be purged, because purging would require identifying the authoring signature, and the authoring signature had been obscured in the falsification."

Nia understood the problem. The falsifier had covered their own authorship. The phrase could be removed from use. The hand could not be named without forcing the record itself to speak.

"The Current considered two remedies. The first was a sustained chemical scrub of the library record, which would take an estimated fifty-seven Thren years and would produce irreversible loss to other records beyond the falsification. The second was the mourning rite, which would force the chamber to name what had been falsified and thereby name its author."

Nia registered that the Sixth had chosen the rite.

She registered, also, that the scrub's cost had been fifty-seven years. Nearly a working life.

"Selathen-of-the-Calm-Reading, a senior teacher of the Sixth Current, offered to perform the rite. Selathen was the speaker whose grief-phrase had been the phrase falsified. The Current agreed. The rite was opened at oh four hundred local on the twenty-ninth day of the eleventh month, in the Sixth Current's consultation chamber, before six witnesses of the Current and one observer of the Third."

Nia stopped.

Selathen's own grief-phrase had been the phrase taken from her. The falsifier had used the speaker's own grief as the raw material of the weapon. Selathen had volunteered to perform the rite that would purify what had been taken from her.

She read on.

"Selathen opened the rite with the three modes intact. She held the first three beats of the mourning sequence cleanly. At the fourth beat her signature began to take the weight of the chamber's response. The Current had assembled the strongest listeners at its disposal, and their responses, which the rite compelled, settled against her body in the standard manner. She did not stop."

Nia thought: she was told not to stop. She did not stop.

"At the seventh beat Selathen began to carry the falsified phrase across the tile island. The phrase had been written for the library, not for performance. It did not sit cleanly in a speaker's body. Witnesses recorded that she held the phrase for three full seconds before she released it into the chamber. The three seconds were recorded as the longest the witnesses had ever seen a Sixth Current speaker hold a signature she had not authored."

Nia breathed out slowly.

"At the ninth beat the falsified phrase began to take its shape in the chamber. The chamber recognized the phrase. The chamber also recognized, because the rite compelled it, the authoring signature that had been obscured in the library. The authoring signature resolved at the tenth beat. The signature was Helvarin-of-the-Outer-Study, a scholar of the Fifth Current on loan to the Sixth's library team in the third year of the post-contact measure. Helvarin was not present at the rite. Helvarin was found in his quarters at the end of the same day, in the posture of final refusal, having taken his own life at an hour not known in the record."

Nia closed her hand.

The falsifier had not waited to be named.

"At the eleventh beat Selathen began the closing. She released the suppressor correctly. She released the held name correctly. Witnesses recorded both as clean. At the twelfth beat Selathen began to lose the carrier of her voice. Her vocalization thinned. Her pigment-glyph held. Her chemical register held. At the thirteenth beat her signature began to fold inward. She was, as the record notes, still performing the closing as her body began to fail."

Nia read the line three times.

Selathen had kept performing. She had held the rite through her own failing.

"At the fourteenth beat Selathen completed the closing. At the fifteenth beat she was no longer holding the three modes as one. Her body could not continue to hold them. Witnesses recorded, in formal notation, the precise signatures of her final twelve seconds. The formal record of those twelve seconds has been sealed by the Current. It has not been made available. It has been named, by the Current, the Teacher's Answer."

Nia did not try to read past the notation. There was nothing to read. The last twelve seconds of Selathen's signature were not in the record. They had been sealed.

"The rite closed. The library was purified of the falsified phrase, which was made to resolve into Helvarin's original authoring components and then to dissolve at the library's margin. The Fifth Current acknowledged the falsification, the falsifier, and the falsifier's failure to answer the rite before it closed on him. No reparation was offered, because the falsifier was dead. No reparation was demanded, because the phrase had been purified. The consultation between the Sixth and the Fifth was reopened eleven months later at the Sixth's invitation and continues to the present."

The Fifth had eventually been invited back. The Sixth had made that choice.

"Selathen-of-the-Calm-Reading is honored in the Sixth Current's private register as a performer of the rite and as the speaker whose grief-phrase was the first Thren grief-phrase to be weaponized in the post-contact era. The Current does not record her death publicly. The Current records her, in the language of the rite, as having answered."

Nia reached the end of the record.

She did not close the file.

She sat with the phrase as having answered. It was not the phrasing she would have expected. It was not a phrasing a human record would have used for a person who had died performing a rite.

The Sixth Current had not recorded Selathen's death. They had recorded her answering.

Nia thought, unbidden, of Vance. Of his hands folding in the posture of open hearing. Of the half-second she had spent on the lie. Of the word answering.

She did not think about what it meant for her yet. She could not.

She read the record again. She read it three times.

She had learned, at some hour in the reading, that the fourth purification was not a piece of history. It was a set of instructions. The Sixth Current had given her, in making the record available, not only the weight of what she was asking to do. It had also given her the shape of a performance that had closed correctly, against a cost she had been told about in the abstract and was now reading in a record.

She had also learned that Selathen had completed the closing. Selathen had not been stopped by her own failing.

Nia understood that this was not meant to comfort her.

Nia understood that it was meant to tell her what was possible.

She closed the record. She saved the phrase, as having answered, into her private notes.

She sat with it.

She had used most of the seventeen minutes.

Her comm pulsed.

Fifteen

Dhillon replied in seventeen minutes.

His message was short. He had arranged a consultation at nineteen hundred, in the lesser chamber, at the Thren request. He would meet her at the air-lock atrium at eighteen forty. He would not be entering the chamber with her.

Nia read it twice. She went to the small closet. She put on the clothes she had been wearing on the ninth day, which she had folded and kept because she had not yet been able to throw them out. She put on the thin suspension undergarment the embassy issued to delegates. She put on the outer layer that flared slightly at the wrists, so it would catch the medium without restricting her hands.

She checked the time. 18:37.

She walked to the air-lock atrium.

Dhillon was already there, in the formal blue-and-grey of the senior civil service, the layer that signaled a Concordance officer on a consultation. He looked at Nia when she came in, and he did not, for once, try to read her face.

"They have agreed to hear you," he said. "That is all they have agreed to."

"All right."

"The First-Speaker will be in the chamber. Vorathan will be with her. There will be one attendant whose standing I could not identify. You will be alone on the human side."

"All right."

"You can still turn around."

"I know."

He nodded. He cycled the inner door. The outer door opened onto the corridor that led to the lesser chamber.

The lesser chamber was a quarter the size of the audience chamber. The suspension volume was five meters by five meters by three meters high, and held a single ceremonial island of tile in the center, large enough for one human speaker. The walls were not transparent. The light was low, calibrated to the warmer end of the Thren spectrum, which rendered human skin in a color Nia had not seen on her own skin before and had only read about in case notes from medical officers who had spent too long in the ceremonial spaces.

She entered the airlock. The airlock cycled. She walked into the suspension.

The medium was the same medium. The warmth was the same warmth. The pressure was the same pressure. Her heart, which she had believed she had readied for this, registered the familiar sensory field and lurched sideways once before she brought it back under.

The First-Speaker was on the far side of the tile island. She was the same First-Speaker who had delivered the closing of the Acceptance of Speech on the ninth day. Nia had not seen her in the flesh since. Her signature was the silver-green Nia had spent the afternoon not thinking about. She was not in her ceremonial posture today. She was in a posture Nia had read about but not seen a speaker perform outside of scholarly reconstructions. It was called, in Nia's notation, the posture of cold listening. It was used by First Current authorities when they had already made up their minds to be disappointed, and were prepared, formally, to be otherwise.

Vorathan was at the First-Speaker's left, half a body-length behind. His limbs were held in attending at an angle. His signature was small and very careful.

The third figure Nia had been told about was in the shadow behind the First-Speaker, in a posture Nia did not know. She did not turn to try to read it.

Nia crossed the volume to the tile island.

She stood.

She had rehearsed what she was going to say for two hours. She did not rehearse it again now. The rehearsal had been for a human ear. The First-Speaker was not a human ear.

She spoke in the three modes at once, which was what standing in the suspension required of any speaker who had the skill to attempt it. Her vocalization was small and precise. Her pigment-patch carried the approximate human glyph for formal request. Her chemical register released, at her throat and cuffs, the small measured compound she had carried in her inside coat pocket: the Thren name of the mourning.

"A speaker stands in the chamber," she said. "She is a speaker of another body, under standing of the Concordance, trained in the grammar of the rite. She asks the First-Speaker to hear her. The hearing she asks is the opening of the mourning."

The First-Speaker did not speak for four full seconds. She did not move. Her signature, silver-green and cold, drifted toward the tile island and lapped against Nia's feet.

Then she spoke in the three modes at once.

Her vocalization was deep, slow, and carried through Nia's teeth. Her pigment-flash moved along her mantle in a pattern that took Nia a second to translate and another second to believe. Her chemical register was an appall.

"You are a speaker of another body," the First-Speaker said.

"I am."

"You are not a Current."

"I am not."

"You are not a family-level speaker of the body you bear."

"I am a child of two cryptographers and a session musician, under the legal kinship of Earth. I stand in the only family I was given."

"The rite was made for ours."

"I know."

"You are asking to carry a weight our speakers do not carry except in extremity."

"I know."

"You are asking this for a speaker of your own body who died inside my chamber."

"Yes."

"The rite, once opened, will not end until the chamber has answered."

"I understand."

"You do not understand. You understand what you have read. The rite is not what you have read."

"I understand that also."

The First-Speaker was silent. Her signature drew close to her, contracting, pigment flashes resolving into a slower pattern Nia had not encountered in any literature.

"Why," the First-Speaker said.

"Because the speech that killed him read as ours. Because the Concordance has now adopted a record that also reads as ours. Because there is no human chamber in which the truth of his death can be made to respond. There is only yours."

The First-Speaker was quiet for a long time.

Vorathan, from his place half a body-length behind her, had not moved or spoken. His signature was held at the edge of what could still be called speech.

The attendant in the shadow had also not moved.

"The rite is held by the speakers," the First-Speaker said. "The speakers are seven. The Fifth will refuse you, because the Fifth is the Current the human record has named, and the Fifth will say that the record is the record. Six may hear you. To perform the rite in a chamber not your own, you must be heard by each of the six, and four of the six must grant consent. Your Concordance will not be permitted to speak for you in these hearings. They are between you and the Currents. If you cannot find four, you cannot perform the rite. If you find four, I will open the chamber to you myself."

"All right."

"You will have until the completion of the seventh day of mourning to find the four. That is the length of time the chamber remains in withdrawn hearing. After the seventh day the silence ends, and once the silence has ended, the rite cannot be performed."

"How long is the day on Sepharu."

"Twenty-eight of your hours."

Nia did the arithmetic quickly. The chamber had entered its withdrawn hearing at the close of the Acceptance, roughly ten hours before. She had six days and eighteen hours before the silence ended.

"I accept," she said.

"You do not accept. You ask."

"I ask."

"I have heard you."

The First-Speaker turned in place, a movement which, in a Thren of her standing, was itself a ritual motion. Her three modes closed in a single signature Nia registered as dismissal-in-formal-register.

The meeting was over.

Nia walked back to the tile island edge, crossed the volume, and entered the airlock. She did not look at Vorathan. She did not look at the attendant in the shadow. She did not look back.

The airlock cycled.

The dry air of the compound took her like a hand.

Dhillon was at the outer door.

"Well," he said.

"Six days and eighteen hours. Four of six Currents to consent. Not the Fifth. Through me, not the service."

"Dear god."

"Vorathan is with me. The First-Speaker will allow the rite if I find the four."

"All right."

"I am going to my quarters."

"Yes. You should."

She walked past him.

She did not think about the six days. She did not think about the four Currents. She thought about the chamber: the smell of the First-Speaker's dismissal, the weight of the attendant's unread posture, Vorathan's silence. She thought about the small measured compound of the mourning name she had released at her throat and her cuffs. It had cost her two of her vials.

She had four left.

Sixteen

The first Current she asked was the Sixth.

Vorathan had been clear, through two chemical exchanges across the garden monitoring in the four hours since the First-Speaker's ruling, that the Sixth Current was the Current she would approach first if she wanted to go in with the best chance of being heard. The Sixth Current was the Current of formal grieving. They understood the rite from the inside. Their senior speakers had been present, in various small capacities, at three of the four recorded performances. They were also, Vorathan had said in a phrase that took Nia ten minutes to decipher, the Current most likely to say no for a reason she would understand.

She had thanked him, chemically.

She had not asked him whether he would be in the room.

She had dressed in the same suspension layer she had worn for the First-Speaker, because it was all she had. She had carried three of her four remaining vials in the inside pocket of her coat. She had left the fourth on her desk. Four Currents would need to hear her name their name formally, and she had only four vials. The math was easy. The math was also unforgiving.

The Sixth Current's consultation chamber was three corridors from the lesser chamber, at the back of the Thren compound where the architecture thinned toward the shoreline. It was older than the audience chamber by three hundred Thren years, which was the kind of fact Nia had read in case notes and had never expected to verify. The walls were shell, layered in the translucent rising spirals the Thren had built with before they had learned the tile work of the modern compound. The suspension volume inside was oblong, narrower than the audience chamber, and the ceiling lower, close enough over the tile island that a Thren of the Sixth Current's full standing would have had to hold themselves carefully not to brush it. The light was green. It was the color of deep water over old shell, not the color of the compound's engineered spectrum, and Nia understood, crossing to the airlock, that the Thren had not updated this chamber's lighting because they did not want to.

She entered at twenty-one oh seven. Her escort waited at the outer corridor. She cycled the airlock alone.

The Thren inside was not Vorathan.

It was a figure Nia had never met, whose signature was a muted amber. Their limbs were held in a posture Nia recognized but had never seen performed outside of ritual diagrams. It was the posture of opened listening, which in the Sixth Current was reserved for grief-conversation. It meant the speaker was prepared to hear, without judgment, anything the petitioner would say, and to respond only in the register of grief itself. It was a courtesy. It was also, in certain readings of Sixth Current literature, a containment.

Nia crossed the volume.

She stood on the tile island at the far side.

"You come to me with the name of the mourning," the Sixth Current speaker said.

"I do."

"You are the human of the ninth day."

"I am."

"You stood beside the one who fell."

"Yes."

"Tell me what he was to you."

Nia had prepared for seventeen versions of this meeting, and had not prepared for that question. She stood in the green light of a chamber older than her doctorate, and she heard her own breath, and she answered.

"He was my ambassador," she said. "He was also my friend. He was a man who had taken the measure of me in nine days, and had decided I could be trusted with him. He was the second person in my professional life who had decided that. He was dead before I could answer him."

The Sixth Current speaker was silent.

Their signature, amber, drew closer across the volume, and settled against Nia's wrists.

"I have heard you," they said.

"You are asking to open the mourning for this one."

"Yes."

"You are not of his Current, because you have no Current. You are not of his body, because you bear your own. You are not of his line, because the line of a human is not the line of a speaker. You are asking to open the mourning for him regardless."

"Yes."

"It is a thing that will not end until the chamber has answered."

"I know."

"It is a thing that will be answered by your own body, because you are the speaker who opens it."

"I know."

The Sixth Current speaker was silent again. Their amber signature was a small slow pulse now, almost tidal in its rhythm.

"I will tell you what I think," they said. "I think the one who fell did not die of the Fifth. I have thought so since the hour he fell, as have all the speakers of my Current, which is why we have grieved and why we have not spoken. I think the one who killed him was a speaker of your own body. I think the rite will find that speaker, because the rite finds what it is called to find. I think your body will not survive opening the rite, because you have not been trained from birth to carry what it casts. I think, if you survive it, the peace may survive. If you do not, you will have bought the peace for the rest of us with a coin the Thren do not know how to repay."

Nia did not speak.

She stood in the green light and let the speaker's amber signature settle, and she registered, because she had been trained to register it, that the speaker had not asked her whether she wanted to proceed. The speaker had assumed she did. The speaker had already moved on to the question of the cost.

"I will grant you my Current's consent," the Sixth Current speaker said. "I will grant it without condition and without qualification, because to condition it would be to pretend the rite is a thing I can shape, and the rite is not. I grant it to you. I will not stand beside you in the chamber. I am not yours to stand beside. I am, after tonight, your witness."

Nia bowed in the small formal human way.

"Thank you," she said.

"Do not thank me," the Sixth Current speaker said. "The rite is not a gift. The rite is a weight. I have agreed to add mine to yours."

The Sixth Current speaker closed their three modes into a farewell signature Nia had read about in two monographs and had not expected to feel. It was warm. It was slow. It carried no trace of the amber listening register that had preceded it. It was something older than judgment. Nia held it on her wrists for as long as the circulation of the suspension allowed, and then she bowed again, and she turned, and she walked back to the airlock.

The airlock cycled.

She crossed the outer corridor in the escort's silent company. She walked back along the three corridors. She came to the lesser chamber's atrium, where Dhillon was not waiting, because Dhillon had returned to the civil service wing. She found Vorathan, alone, in the posture of attending at an angle.

He did not speak. She did not speak.

She held up one finger.

The Sixth Current had consented.

Vorathan cycled one slow pulse of his signature, which Nia, after two days of reading him, understood as the Thren equivalent of a grin of relief.

Then he turned. She followed. They walked toward the Fourth.

Seventeen

They walked the length of the Thren compound in silence.

Vorathan walked three paces ahead. In the convention of his Current, this was the correct distance for a scholar escorting a petitioner whose hearing his Current had not yet agreed to grant. It was also the distance at which no Thren watching could claim he had taken her arm or offered her support. Nia understood both meanings. She did not close the gap.

The Fourth Current's chamber was not in the ceremonial quarter. It was in the scholars' range, which was a long low building the Thren had attached to the compound in the decade since contact specifically so that Fourth Current scholars could receive outside petitioners without requiring the rest of the Current to participate. The building had fewer suspension volumes than any of the other Current chambers Nia had read about. The Fourth Current did not grieve in public. They argued in private.

A junior scholar passed them going the other way, carrying slates. Their signature lifted in a small formal courtesy to Vorathan: three beats, a pause, a fourth, another pause, a fifth. It was an eccentric rhythm Nia had read about once, in an early-contact survey, as a rare developmental variant some scholars kept rather than smoothed out. The junior did not look at her. Vorathan returned the courtesy without slowing.

The airlock was at the end of a narrow corridor. Vorathan stopped before it. He turned.

"The speaker is Nemari-of-the-Long-Reading," he said, quietly, through the air of the corridor rather than the suspension. "She is not an elder. She is not a judge. She is the most senior scholar the Current agreed to put forward on this hearing. She is also the scholar whose last paper I cited in the third of my own dissertations. She has not forgiven me for that citation."

Nia did not ask why.

"Be precise," Vorathan said. "Do not speak of grief. Speak of meaning."

"All right."

"She will not like me being here."

"All right."

He cycled the airlock.

The suspension inside was narrow and tall, the opposite of the Sixth Current's oblong. The tile island was a bare post, waist-high, that a standing human would have to lean against rather than stand on. The light was a cold bone-white. It rendered Nia's skin bloodless. It rendered the Thren in the chamber, who was Nemari-of-the-Long-Reading, in a register of indigo Nia had never read before and would not have translated correctly on a first encounter. She stood at the post and she waited to be addressed.

Nemari did not move when Vorathan entered the chamber. She did not move when he took his place in the formal subordinate posture of a junior Fourth Current scholar in the presence of a senior, which was a posture Nia had watched him practice in passing at the lesser chamber and had not understood at the time. Nemari's signature was tight and flat. It was held at the center of her body in a small contained pulse. It was the signature of a speaker who had already prepared her remarks.

"You have come to me with the name of the mourning," Nemari said.

"I have."

"You have come with Vorathan-of-the-Gathering-Dusk, who is a scholar of this Current under my review, and whose involvement in your matter is already noted."

Nia had not known it was noted. She had suspected. She did not say so.

"I note it," she said.

"You do not. The noting is mine. The noting is not yours. You understand the distinction."

"I do."

"Speak."

Nia had rehearsed the Fourth Current version of her address on the walk down the compound. It was shorter than the Sixth Current version. It contained no words for family. It contained no words for loss. It contained a single claim about meaning, in three modes.

She spoke. Her vocalization was careful. Her pigment-patch carried the human glyph for a scholar's petition. Her chemical register released, at her throat, a phrase Nemari would know, because Nemari had written about it in her fifth paper.

"A meaning has been falsified," Nia said. "A falsified meaning has killed a speaker of my body. The chamber in which he was killed is the Thren chamber. The rite that was made to compel a chamber to answer is the rite held by the seven speakers. I ask the Fourth Current, which has been the first Current to treat meaning as the matter, to grant consent to the opening of that rite."

Nemari held her signature for nine seconds.

Then she said: "No."

Nia stood still.

"The Fourth Current will not grant consent," Nemari said, "because the Fourth Current's concern is the integrity of meaning itself, and the rite is not a tool for the correction of a meaning-falsification inside another body. The rite is not an instrument. You are treating it as an instrument. The First-Speaker has indulged your proposal because the First Current's concern is the peace. The Sixth Current has consented because the Sixth Current's concern is the grief. The Fourth Current's concern is neither. We do not lend our standing to rites we believe are being used as tools. We do not lend our standing to rites we believe should not be opened for causes that are not ours. I have heard you. I refuse."

Nia did not argue.

She had prepared three arguments. None of them addressed what Nemari had just said.

"I have heard you," she said.

"You have. You may leave."

Nia turned toward the airlock. She paused. She turned back.

"Senior Scholar," she said. "Vorathan's involvement."

Nemari held her signature steady.

"Is under review," she said. "The Fourth Current will decide the consequence on the seventh day of mourning, at the close of the silence. Vorathan knows this. Vorathan has known it for eighteen hours. His continued involvement in your matter is his own decision, not my Current's. That decision is what my Current is reviewing."

Vorathan did not speak.

Nia bowed in the small formal human way.

She left the chamber.

The airlock cycled. The dry air of the corridor was colder than she had left it. Vorathan walked three paces ahead until they reached the junction that would split, and then he stopped.

He turned. He looked at her. He did not speak for a moment.

"I am going back to the scholars' range," he said. "I am going to sit with my Current through the decision of the next six days. That is the thing I can do. It is not the thing I would do if I could do otherwise, but it is the thing my Current permits me to do while they review."

"Vorathan."

"You will go to the First next. The First will be easier than the Fourth. The First-Speaker has already indulged you. She will either grant you her Current's consent now, or ask you a question for which you must answer at the Thren cost. I have written a note for you. It is in the scholars' range archive, tagged under your credentials. You can read it from your terminal."

"All right."

"Iyana."

She looked up. He had not used her given name.

"Do not save me from the Current's decision. That is not yours to do. The Current's decision is mine."

"All right."

He turned and walked back down the corridor.

Nia walked back through the compound to her quarters.

She was not stopped. She was not followed. She had been given a junior officer for the Sixth Current walk. The officer had returned her here. Now the officer was gone. That meant somebody in the civil service had decided to let her finish the Current circuit without chaperone, which meant somebody in the civil service was watching how it went.

She did not stop to consider who.

She went into her quarters. She closed the door. She sat at the desk.

One yes. One no. Four Currents left. She needed three of them.

She opened the terminal.

Eighteen

She opened Vorathan's note at twenty-three oh six.

It was in the scholars' range archive under her credentials, which was a system she had not known her credentials reached. She opened the archive with the faint professional irritation she still felt whenever a colleague turned out to know more about the structure of the Concordance academic systems than she did. The file was marked private, sealed to her signature, and named with a Thren glyph Nia had to look up before she could even pronounce it. It rendered approximately as notes-for-a-speaker-whose-hearing-is-not-yet-complete. The Thren compression was tighter than her notation could reproduce.

The note ran four pages.

The First Current, it said, would not grant her consent at the first hearing. The First-Speaker had already heard her proposal, already ruled, and already committed the First Current to the posture of indulging her approach to the other Currents. For the First to grant consent now would be to commit before the Fourth, the Second, the Third, and the Seventh had spoken. The First-Speaker would therefore ask her a question whose purpose was to defer decision without appearing to defer. The question would be, in form, about Nia's preparation. The First-Speaker would ask whether Nia had eaten of the mourning bread. Nia would not have eaten of it. She would not yet know what it was. The question was a formality that established the First would grant consent if and when Nia had completed a physical preparation. The physical preparation was the mourning fast: sixty hours without food, broken only by bread baked by a Sixth Current grief-speaker and offered by her at the close of the sixtieth hour. Nia, Vorathan wrote, would need to begin the fast tonight if she wanted the First Current's consent before the seventh day.

Nia read that paragraph three times.

She did the arithmetic. She had six days and roughly fourteen hours left, which was one hundred and eighty-two hours. If she began the fast tonight and broke it at the sixtieth hour, she would break it with one hundred and twenty-two hours still on the clock, which was enough to perform the rite and to attempt the Second, Third, and Seventh Currents' hearings in whatever order she could manage. The math was not impossible. The math was also not gentle.

The Second Current, Vorathan wrote, was the Current most likely to grant consent on pragmatic grounds. They were not ritualists. They were not philosophers. They were administrators, and they cared about what any action cost the peace. The Second would ask Nia what the refusal of her proposal would cost. She should be prepared to answer with a number. The Second understood costs in numbers. They would not understand costs in any other register.

The Third Current, Vorathan wrote, was the Current Nia would have the hardest time reading. The Third had retreated into sealed meditation volumes on the day Vance had fallen, and they were in sealed meditation still. To address the Third, Nia would have to enter the sealed volume herself. She would be permitted to speak. She would not be permitted to see the speakers who heard her. The Third would decide after she left. Their decision could take hours or days.

The Seventh Current, Vorathan wrote, had gone quiet on the day Vance fell and had not spoken to any other Current since. The Concordance assumed the Seventh was hiding, which was the Concordance's word. The correct word was not hiding. The correct word in the Thren grammar was neither a verb nor a noun. The Seventh had made themselves unavailable to speech. They had a reason the other Currents were not permitted to ask about. If Nia tried to find them, she would not find them. If the Seventh wanted to hear her, they would find her. Vorathan could not predict when, or whether, or how.

The note ended with three words in Vorathan's own private notation that rendered, approximately, as: you can win this.

Nia sat at the desk for a long moment after she closed the file.

She understood several things at once.

She had a fast to begin, which meant she should not have the meal she was already thinking about having. She had a Second Current meeting to prepare for with a specific kind of answer, which meant she needed to do math she had not done yet. She had a Third Current meeting she could not prepare for, because she would not see her audience. She had a Seventh Current meeting that could not be arranged and could only be waited on. And she had a First Current consent that was already hers if she could survive sixty hours without food.

That was five Currents of outcome to sort across a hundred and fifty-odd remaining hours, which was the kind of arithmetic a student of hers would have found intimidating, and which Nia, at thirty-one, found clarifying. She did the kind of planning she had been trained to do: make a list in her head, assign probabilities, do the earliest one.

She began the fast at twenty-three twelve.

She went into the galley alcove. She opened the cooling drawer. She took out the remaining meal she had not finished two days earlier, and she threw it away without opening it. She drank a glass of water. She went back to the desk.

She wrote a short message to Dhillon. It said she would be unavailable for the next sixty hours for reasons she would explain in person at the end of them. She wrote a second message to the embassy infirmary, logging a scholarly fast for Thren ceremonial purposes under her junior linguist credentials. The infirmary would not approve the fast. They would note it. They would send a medical technician to check on her twice during the sixty hours. That was procedure. She did not object to it.

She checked the time. 23:19.

She did not message Ilsia. She did not message Adrian. She considered both and put both aside.

She thought about the Second Current question. What would the refusal of her proposal cost? She thought about it for seventeen minutes. She wrote two numbers in her private notes. The first was the count of human worlds the Thren peace currently covered: forty. The second was the number of Thren lifetimes the peace represented across the Seven Currents, roughly twelve, since each Thren lifetime was longer than a human one. She did not yet know how to turn the numbers into an answer the Second Current would accept. She would keep thinking.

She looked at her bed.

She did not go to it.

She sat at the desk with her hands folded and she closed her eyes. She was not going to sleep yet. She wanted to sit with the shape of the day behind her before she let it go. She had asked for the mourning in the lesser chamber. She had been consented to by the Sixth Current in the shell chamber at the back of the compound. She had been refused by the Fourth Current in the scholars' range.

Vorathan had called her Iyana. That was the name her mother had used. It was also the name Nia had stopped answering to in her doctoral years, because her advisor had been bad at pronouncing it, and the bad pronunciation had hurt to hear.

She sat for a long time.

At twenty-three fifty-one she stood. She went to the bed. She lay down. She did not sleep at first. The fast was loud in her stomach, which she had not expected, and the silence of the compound was louder than she had registered before. Eventually she slept.

When she went to sleep, she had one hundred and fifty-nine hours left.

Nineteen

The medical technician came at seven-thirty.

She was a Concordance corporal Nia had not met before, young, efficient. She cycled the door, introduced herself, took Nia's pulse and temperature in the same gesture, noted them in a small instrument at her belt, asked what hour the fast had begun, noted that as well, and asked if Nia was aware of the standard early-fast symptoms. Nia said she was. The corporal said she would return in ten hours. Nia said she understood. The corporal left.

Nia sat on the edge of the bed for a long moment.

The fast was nine hours old. It was a weight in her stomach that was not entirely hunger and not entirely discipline, sitting where her breakfast would have been. Her tongue tasted of nothing. Her pulse had been two beats faster than her baseline, which the corporal had not commented on and which Nia had registered the way a linguist registers a grammatical anomaly. A second-day fast was meant to produce three symptoms, taught in the Concordance infirmary literature in the order one could expect them: raised heart rate, tongue dullness, and a short interval of visual sharpening that felt like clarity and was not. She had the first two. She waited for the third.

She stood up. She drank water. She opened the terminal.

She spent two hours with the numbers.

She had come to the terminal expecting to build the model from first principles and had found, in the first ten minutes, that she was not going to have to. The Concordance-Thren shared record already contained eleven years of incident data, categorized by cause and outcome, with a standard disengagement-model library the Concordance economic research office had been maintaining since before contact. She had used that library once during her postdoc and had found it clumsy. She found it competent now. Her part of the work was picking the right scenario, picking the right two precedents, and deciding which of her own twelve assumptions she was prepared to defend to a Thren administrator.

By ten hundred she had an answer.

It was imperfect, but it was specific. She had modeled the cost of refusal across three Thren years, using the last eleven years of incident data from the shared record, adjusted for a worsened-relations scenario she had extrapolated from the two most similar cases in the human diplomatic literature: the Martian disengagement of the twenty-one forties, and the Coalition-breakdown models from the pre-Gate era. She had arrived at a figure that rose and fell by several percent depending on her assumptions, and that rounded to one hundred and fourteen.

One hundred and fourteen additional deaths across both species across three Thren years.

Also, three to five human colonies likely to withdraw from active peace cooperation, and one Thren Current likely to pull back from diplomatic engagement.

She saved the model. She closed the terminal.

She dressed.

The escort at her door was not the junior officer who had walked her to the Sixth. It was a new officer, older, male, also neutral. He introduced himself with only a last name, Pryce, confirmed her destination as the Second Current's working chamber in the Thren compound east wing, and waited while she put on her coat.

She took two vials. She took the notebook with the model in it. She took a cup of water, which she had been told was the only thing she was permitted during the fast.

They walked.

The Second Current's working chamber was a long low room with a suspension volume in the center and a row of small working alcoves along one wall. The alcoves had slate surfaces and writing tools. The suspension volume was small, maybe four meters across, with no tile island at all. Petitioners, Nia realized with a faint human frustration, were expected to stand directly on the chamber floor. It was a detail Vorathan had not mentioned. She registered it. She would stand.

There were three Thren in the chamber. One was in the suspension volume, at its center, in a working posture Nia had not seen in the field but had read about. It was called, in Thren scholarship, the posture of the kept count: limbs slightly lowered, signature folded tight, the attention of a Thren reading a ledger. The other two Thren were in the alcoves, at slate surfaces, writing. They did not look up when Nia entered. They did not, in the convention of the Second Current, need to.

She entered the suspension. She walked to the center of the volume.

The suspension was warmer than she had expected, or perhaps she was colder than she had realized. Without the tile island under her feet, the buoyancy of the medium took her slightly: the floor was there but her weight was not quite on it. She did not shift. She did not lean. She stood where a Thren did not expect a human to be able to stand, and she waited.

The Thren in the posture of the kept count opened their signature just enough to be heard.

"Ostren-of-the-Given-Count," they said. "You have come with the name of the mourning."

"I have."

"What does refusal of your proposal cost?"

Nia did not answer in three modes. This was not that kind of chamber.

"One hundred and fourteen," she said.

Ostren held their signature still.

"Across what."

"Three Thren years. One hundred and fourteen deaths across both species. Three to five human colonies likely to withdraw from active peace cooperation. One Thren Current likely to pull back from diplomatic engagement."

"How."

"The last eleven years of incident data from the Concordance-Thren shared record, extrapolated to a worsened-relations scenario using two precedents in the human diplomatic literature."

"Which precedents."

"The Martian disengagement of the twenty-one forties. The Coalition-breakdown models from the pre-Gate era."

"Your model has assumptions."

"It has twelve."

"Which is the assumption most likely to be wrong."

"That the pre-Gate Coalition-breakdown models apply to a post-Gate contact relationship. Gate-era diplomacy has different decay functions. If that assumption is wrong, the number is lower by roughly thirty-one percent."

"Eighty, then."

"Eighty-four."

"Eighty-four is still a number."

"Yes."

Ostren was silent for a long moment. Their signature did not change. The two Thren in the alcoves continued to write.

"The Second Current grants consent," Ostren said.

They did not ornament the statement. They said it the way a ledger entry was made.

Nia did not move. She had prepared to argue. She had prepared counter-arguments to three possible Second Current objections she had worked through in her head during the walk. None of them was relevant now.

"Thank you," she said.

"You do not need to thank me. You have given me a number that has the shape of a number. If your number had been bad, or if you had not had a number, the Second Current would have refused on grounds of insufficient rigor. You had a number. We have granted consent. That is the transaction."

"I understand."

"You are in the second day of the mourning."

"Yes."

"You are fasting."

"Yes."

"You will be in the First Current's chamber at the end of the sixtieth hour."

"Yes."

"Good."

Ostren closed their three modes in a small dismissal signature Nia registered as end-of-ledger-entry, the Thren equivalent of a form being filed and set aside. The meeting was over.

Nia walked back out through the airlock. The medical technician's check-in from earlier sat in her comm as a neutral line of text noting her vitals. Pryce was waiting in the outer corridor. He nodded once when she emerged and asked, in the formal phrasing of a service escort, where she was going next.

"Quarters," she said.

They walked. At the junction of the east wing and the residential corridor, the third symptom arrived: the short interval of visual sharpening that felt like clarity and was not. The embassy lighting took on a thin edge. The pattern of the corridor tiles resolved in her peripheral vision with unnatural precision. She walked through it. She knew what it was. She would not trust what it told her.

Two yeses. One no. Three Currents left. She needed two of them.

The Third Current was next, in the sealed meditation volume, where she would speak and not see who heard her.

Twenty

Pryce walked her to the Third Current's threshold and stopped.

The threshold was a plain arch set into a stone wall that had been polished flat over two hundred Thren years of use. There was no airlock in the usual sense. There was a door of rising layered shell, like the Sixth Current's walls but thicker and less translucent, and a single chemical seal along its base that no Concordance technician had ever been permitted to examine. Nia had read about this door on day three of her orientation, in a paragraph written by a scholar who had not been able to cross it.

"I can't follow you past this," Pryce said.

"I know."

"If you come out before two hours, the medical tech is to be at your door."

"I know."

"If you do not come out at all."

"There is a protocol for that."

"I memorized it."

"Of course you did."

She did not smile. He did not expect her to. He stepped back and folded his hands behind him. He became, formally, a pillar.

Nia approached the door.

The door did not open for her. The chemical seal recognized her only at the moment she breathed directly against it, a detail Vorathan's note had not mentioned and which she realized, as it happened, was a Third Current test. She stood at the door. She breathed. The seal recognized her. The door opened.

She walked in.

The Third Current's sealed meditation volume was dark.

It was not the dark of the compound's night cycle, which the embassy designers had calibrated to approximate Earth winter night. It was a dark older than calibration. It was a dark the Third Current had agreed upon, at some point in their architectural history, to be the correct dark for the purpose. The ceiling and walls did not reflect any part of the human visual spectrum. The air glowed, very faintly, with the ambient bioluminescence of the suspension medium itself, because the medium was engineered to hold a low signal that let chemically sensitive beings orient. To a human eye, the glow rendered distance as depth without contour.

Nia stood inside the threshold and let her eyes adjust. After a long moment, she saw the shape of the volume.

It was concentric.

Three rings of floor, each lower than the one outside it by a hand's breadth. The outer ring was where she was. The middle ring ran around the center, wider than the outer, containing what looked, in the dim signal-glow, like rows of seated Thren in meditation postures. She could not make out their signatures. Their bioluminescence had been damped, another Third Current practice whose rationale Vorathan's note had not explained and which Nia now understood as the practical expression of the Third's refusal to be seen by the petitioner. The inner ring, at the center, was a single low pool of deeper darkness. Nia could not see into it at all.

She did not try.

She walked forward one step onto the outer ring.

She stood.

She had prepared a Third Current address on the walk. It was, following Vorathan's counsel, shorter than the Sixth Current version and longer than the Fourth Current version. It was not about grief. It was not about meaning. It was about the question the Third Current asked of any action: whether the action was true to the thing it was done for.

She spoke, in the three modes.

Her vocalization was low and steady, aimed not at any particular hearer but at the volume itself. Her pigment-patch rendered the glyph for a petitioner-in-meditation, which was the Thren glyph closest to the meditative register the Third used. Her chemical register released, very slowly, her third vial.

"A speaker fell in the ninth-day chamber," she said. "He was killed by a speech that was not speech. The speech was made to read as yours. The record of his death is being made to read as yours. I ask to perform the mourning rite, because the rite will not lie. The rite will find what the rite is called to find. I am not of your body. I am not of your Current. I am asking to speak the rite because I believe, in my own field, that the rite is the true answer to the false speech that killed him. I am asking the

Third Current to grant consent on the only grounds the Third Current grants consent: whether the thing I am proposing is true to the thing it is done for."

She stopped.

She listened.

The volume was silent.

No signature rose from the middle ring.

No pigment-flash moved in the inner pool.

She had been told, by Vorathan, that this would be the shape of the hearing. She stood in the silence for what she judged to be sixty seconds. She bowed in the small formal human way, in the direction of the middle ring. She turned.

She walked out.

The door closed behind her. The chemical seal sealed. Pryce was at his pillar position in the corridor. She did not look at him.

"Doctor."

"Yes."

"Your quarters."

"Yes."

They walked.

Nia did not speak on the return. Her body was in the nineteenth hour of the fast and the chamber had been cold, which she now understood was also deliberate. The Third Current did not warm their meditation volume for petitioners. They assumed a petitioner who was speaking truly would not feel the cold. She had felt it. She did not know what that meant for her standing with the Third. She would know when they decided.

Pryce brought her to her door. She went in. She drank water. She sat at the desk.

She did not turn on the terminal. She did not open the comm. She did not model anything. She did not read. She sat with her hands in her lap and she waited, the way she had been told to wait, the way the Third Current required a petitioner to wait.

The second medical technician came at seventeen-thirty.

She was not the same corporal as the morning. She took Nia's pulse and temperature, noted that the pulse was now seven beats above baseline, noted that the tongue was dry, asked about visual sharpening. Nia confirmed it. The corporal said the third-symptom interval was typically six to eight hours. Nia said she understood. The corporal said she would be back in ten hours. Nia said she understood. The corporal left.

Nia drank water.

She sat.

The terminal chimed at twenty-one eleven.

It was not the alert she had set on the garden monitoring. It was a formal diplomatic notice, routed through the Concordance embassy, tagged with the Third Current's working seal.

The Third Current would not grant consent.

The notice was two paragraphs long. The first paragraph said the Third Current had heard her petition in the meditation volume at twelve-fourteen local. The second paragraph said that after eight hours and fifty-seven minutes of deliberation, the Third Current had concluded the rite as Nia proposed it was not true to the thing the rite was done for. The Third Current acknowledged the death of Ambassador Vance. The Third Current acknowledged the forged speech. The Third Current declined to consent to the opening of the rite on the grounds that the rite was not, in the Third Current's understanding, an answer to a forged speech. The rite was an answer to grief within the Thren body. Nia was not of the Thren body. The rite she proposed would, in the Third Current's judgment, fail to find what she called it to find, because what she was calling it to find was human. The Third Current wished her well. The Third Current returned to sealed meditation.

Nia read the notice twice.

She did not cry.

She did not eat. She could not. The fast was on the nineteenth hour, and there was no meal she could have reached for that would have been permitted.

She sat with the notice for a long time.

Two yeses. Two nos. Two Currents left. She needed both.

The Seventh had not been found. The Seventh could not be sought.

The First was waiting at the end of the sixtieth hour.

She opened the terminal. She looked at the time. 21:17. She had forty-one more hours of fast.

She closed the terminal. She went to the bed. She lay down.

She did not sleep.

Twenty-One

She had spent the night at the desk.

She had not opened the terminal after twenty-three seventeen. She had not written anything. She had not eaten, which was the rule. She had drunk water and nothing else. She had sat in the chair with her hands folded and she had thought, in the way a person thinks when they have not yet accepted that there is nothing more to do. At oh four hundred she had recognized that the thinking was not useful. At oh four oh nine she had continued thinking anyway.

At oh six hundred the simulated sky shifted toward the dawn cycle. The compound did not care whether she had slept.

She turned on the terminal.

She checked the garden alert.

Nothing.

She checked the monitoring portal with a broader filter. She checked the history of the past twelve hours in three registers. There was nothing from the Seventh. There was nothing from anyone. Vorathan had not released another signature since his four-signature reply on the first day. His Current had him in review. His review had not ended.

She sat for a long moment.

Then she did the thing she had been trained to do in the presence of stalled waiting, which was to open her own notes.

She opened the chemistry file first.

She reread her own time-stamp on the poison's arrival. She reread the seven matching features and the thirteen non-matching features. She reread Vorathan's four signatures and her own decoded notation for each. She reread her model from yesterday, which had produced the one-hundred-and-fourteen number the Second Current had accepted. She read each file the way she had been taught to reread her own work during her doctoral defense, which was to assume she had been wrong about something and to look for what.

She was not wrong about anything.

That was itself a problem. A scholar who had reread her own case and found no errors was a scholar who had stopped reading carefully, not a scholar whose case was perfect. Nia understood this. She continued reading anyway, because it was what she could do at oh six thirty on the third morning of a fast she could not break.

At oh seven forty-two she found a thing.

It was in the record of the four historical performances of the mourning rite, which she had read three times in her seminar paper and four times in Vorathan's library and twice in her own rereading since he had sent his note. She had been reading it, each time, as a history of the rite. This time she read it as a history of who had been present.

The Seventh Current had not been at any of them.

Not as speaker. Not as witness. Not as listener in a concentric ring. Not as an attendant in any of the records the Concordance library contained. Nia had to go back to her original seminar paper to confirm what she thought she was seeing, and when she did she found that she had noted the absence in a footnote at twenty-six, and had not understood what the footnote meant, and had not thought about the footnote again.

The Seventh had a standing relationship with the mourning rite that consisted of not being present for it.

She sat with that.

It meant one of two things.

The first possibility was that the Seventh did not participate in the mourning rite at all, in which case her need to be heard by the Seventh was an architectural anomaly in the First-Speaker's ruling that Vorathan had not addressed in his note. Vorathan either had not noticed the anomaly, which was unlikely given his Current and his scholarship, or had noticed it and chosen not to tell her, which was more likely for reasons she could not yet see. If the Seventh did not participate, perhaps she did not need their consent. Perhaps the First-Speaker's four-of-six was actually four-of-five, and Nia currently stood at two-yes-two-no and needed only the First. She thought about the First-Speaker. She thought about the silver-green signature on her ankles in the lesser chamber. She thought about the First-Speaker's line about indulging her approach. If she had the First, and she would have the First, because she would survive the fast, then she had the rite.

The second possibility was that the Seventh's absence from the historical rites was itself a form of consent. The Thren had an old grammar for presence-as-participation and absence-as-refusal, which Nia had read about in the same Obi-Halloran seminar that had introduced her to the rite. In that grammar, a Current that was absent from a rite it had a right to witness was a Current that had declined to hear. Such a Current's absence was read as a standing refusal. If this was the framework the Seventh was operating in, Nia had already been refused by them.

Both possibilities suggested the same practical step. Proceed to the First.

The trouble was that she did not know which possibility was correct. She did not know how to find out without speaking to a Thren scholar whose Current was not reviewing him for talking to her.

She considered whether to release a chemical signature in the garden asking Vorathan about this.

She considered it for ten minutes.

She did not release it.

The release would require one of her two remaining vials. It would cost Vorathan more with his Current if he answered. It would force him, if he did answer, to make a scholarly determination about the Seventh Current's legal-ritual status at a moment when his own Current was measuring how much he was willing to compromise his standing for her. It would not get her an answer she could rely on in time.

She closed the chemistry file.

The fast was in its thirtieth hour.

Her pulse was nine beats above her baseline. Her tongue was tacking against the roof of her mouth in a way that felt like paper. The visual-sharpening interval had come and gone twice since yesterday's walk, each time lasting about seven minutes, each time leaving her slightly less oriented when it ended. The literature had said this would stabilize. The literature had said she would adapt.

Nia read the literature the way a linguist reads a translation: as a good-faith attempt at a meaning no one who had not spoken the original had ever fully carried.

She drank water.

She opened the Thirdwater paper one more time. She did not find anything new. The paper was what it was. It was a blueprint. It was a confession. It was eight months old. It would be eight months old tomorrow.

She closed it.

The medical technician at oh nine thirty was a third corporal, an older woman Nia had not expected. She took Nia's vitals with more care than the previous two, looked at the readouts for a long moment, and then said, in a voice Nia found unfamiliar because it was not the service voice: "Dr. Okafor-Reyes, this fast is going to hurt more tomorrow than today. I want you to understand that."

"I understand."

"The third interval has come twice already."

"Yes."

"It is supposed to come three times total. The third is the worst. You will not be able to trust your eyes for about thirty minutes. You will want to act on what you see. Do not act."

"I won't."

"If you need me, my comm is routed to the infirmary duty line. I will come. I will not bring food."

"I know."

"Good."

The corporal left.

Nia sat alone in the quarters with the fast and with the waiting. She realized, somewhere near eleven hundred, that the mental work she had done that morning had not actually changed anything. She had found a pattern. She had thought through two readings of it. She had chosen not to act on either. The pattern could be useful later. For the next six to ten hours, while she waited for the Seventh who might not come, it was not useful.

She closed her eyes.

She did not sleep. She let herself rest.

At fifteen hundred the simulated sky was on the warm gold of weekend afternoon.

At seventeen hundred it had begun its evening shift.

At nineteen hundred the medical tech was back. She took Nia's vitals. She did not speak. She left.

At twenty-one hundred Nia ate nothing and drank water.

At twenty-three hundred she went to the bed.

She lay down.

She did not sleep at first. When she did, it was not sleep. It was a thin state the fast produced that she had read about and had not entirely believed in, where the body rested in the way a body rested and the mind continued, a little, behind the eyes.

The Seventh had not come.

She had, when she stopped counting, one hundred and forty-two hours left.

Twenty-Two

At eleven forty-three the third interval began.

She had been at the desk for six hours, doing nothing she could afterward describe. The morning medical technician had come at oh nine, taken her vitals, noted the worsened pulse and the deeper tongue dullness, and said, more quietly than the corporal the day before, that the third interval was likely today. Nia had said she understood. The corporal had said she would be routed to priority response until the fast ended. Nia had said thank you. The corporal had left.

Between the corporal's visit and eleven forty-three, Nia had done two things. She had reread Vorathan's four signatures one more time. She had drunk water at the standard intervals.

The third interval began as a thin edge along the baseboards, as it had the day before. Then the edge thickened. Then the baseboards themselves became too sharp.

She understood what was happening.

She did not try to move.

The young Thren appeared to her at eleven forty-nine.

Nia did not see them come in. She registered that they were in the room the way a person registers the presence of a cat: with the shift of peripheral attention and no clear point of entry. The young Thren was standing at the edge of the desk. They were small, for a Thren: smaller than Vorathan, smaller than the Sixth Current speaker, smaller than the figures in the meditation volume's middle ring. Their signature was not amber, not silver-green, not indigo. It was a signature Nia had never read in the field or in the literature, and she could not, in the interval's clarity that was not clarity, decide whether she was failing to read it or whether it was failing to be read.

They did not speak for a long moment.

Then they said: "What is the name of the one who fell."

Nia answered.

"Ambassador Teodoro Vance."

"What is the name of the one who will be found."

"I do not know his name in your grammar. His name in mine is Adrian Cho."

"What is your own name."

"Iyana Okafor-Reyes."

The young Thren considered this.

"You are the speaker who would open the mourning."

"Yes."

"You are not of our body."

"No."

"You are speaking into a chamber older than your own."

"Yes."

"Tell me why we should hear you."

Nia sat for a moment. The interval was sharpening everything around the young Thren and nothing about the young Thren themselves, which was a detail she did not pause to register as anomalous. She spoke.

"Because I am the one who saw him fall. Because I am the one who heard the color that killed him and read it as speech. Because I was taught by my mother that every mind that can speak has the right to be heard, and by my father that every code can, in principle, be broken, and by my own teachers that the difference between a cipher and a language is whether someone is willing to be understood. The speech that killed him was a cipher. I am asking your Current to let me translate it into a language, and to let the chamber that was its first audience respond to the translation. I believe this is what the rite is for. I do not know if I am right. I am asking because I do not know. The people who could tell me whether I am right are the people who are not in the chamber. I believe your Current is the Current that made itself absent from the chamber for a reason I have not read in any book but which is starting to feel, in my body, like the reason I need you now."

She had not known she was going to say any of that.

The young Thren was silent for a longer moment.

"That is an answer," they said.

"I know."

"It is not a finished answer."

"No."

"Will you accept our hearing."

"Yes."

"You have it."

The baseboards softened. The thin edge along them retreated. The young Thren was not in the room.

The door to her quarters was open.

She sat in the chair and she did not stand up for a full minute.

She looked at the door. The door was open the way a door is open when it has been opened from the inside: standing a third of the way back, not pulled all the way against the wall. The hinges were not moving. The corridor beyond it was empty. The junior officer who had been her daytime escort was not at his post.

She was not, in the clarity after the interval, confident that any of the last several minutes had happened.

The young Thren had not moved the way a Thren moved. Their signature had not read the way a Thren signature read. She had not heard the airlock at the residential corridor cycle before or after. She had not heard the door open.

She had, possibly, stood up and crossed the room during the interval, opened the door, sat back down, and not remembered any of it. That was a thing the corporal had warned her could happen in the third interval. Nia had told the corporal she would not. She had perhaps done it anyway.

Or she had not.

She did not know.

She stood up. She crossed to the door. She put her hand on the frame.

The frame was cool. The doorway carried no residue of a Thren signature. A Thren who had been there for eight minutes would have left one. The lack of residue could mean no Thren had been in the doorway. It could also mean the Thren had been careful or had been of a

Current that did not leave residue, or had, in the way the Seventh was said to do, made themselves unavailable to the record. Nia understood, standing at the frame, that the whole of her expertise was not going to tell her which of those was true.

She closed the door.

She went back to the desk.

She drank water.

She opened her private notes.

She wrote, in her notation: third interval at 11:43. Duration approximately six minutes. Content: consultation with a young Thren, unidentifiable Current. Content recorded as perceived. Content may be false.

Then she wrote: door found open at end of interval.

She closed the notes.

She was in the forty-fourth hour of the fast.

She had either been heard by the Seventh Current or had hallucinated being heard by them, and she did not know which, and she was not going to know which in the next sixteen hours, and she had to walk to the First-Speaker's chamber in sixteen hours regardless.

She thought, in the clarity after the clarity that was not clarity, that this was probably, now that she considered it, exactly what the Seventh Current wanted her to think.

She opened the terminal.

She set a new alert, this one on her own quarters' door-state log, which had a threshold-level audit no Concordance officer above her rank routinely examined. She backtracked twelve minutes. She pulled the record.

The door had opened at eleven forty-nine.

It had stayed open for six minutes and fourteen seconds.

It had not logged a person passing through in either direction.

She read the entry twice.

She closed the terminal.

She sat with her hands folded and she waited for the fast to continue to end.

Twenty-Three

She startled awake at the knock.

She had not known she was asleep. She had been sitting at the desk, in the thin state the fast produced, which was not rest and was not sleep, and the knock came three times, softly, from her door. She sat up. Her hand went to the desk for balance. Her body registered the sixtieth hour of the fast the way a body registers a long distance it has just finished running, which was to say it was present and it was not entirely hers.

She stood up. She walked to the door. She opened it.

Dhillon was in the corridor.

He was not in the formal blue-and-grey. He was in a plain civilian coat she had not seen him in before, which she registered, in the thin clarity of the sixtieth hour, as a choice. Beside him was a Thren Nia did not immediately recognize, whose signature was a soft unornamented brown, whose limbs were held in the posture of an offering-at-rest. They were a grief-speaker of the Sixth Current. They were carrying something wrapped in a cloth.

"Doctor," Dhillon said.

"Yes."

"The fast is over."

"Yes."

"I am walking you to the First."

"Yes."

"Will you eat first."

"Yes."

The grief-speaker unwrapped the cloth. Inside was a small round loaf of bread, dense and dark, still warm in a way that suggested it had been baked inside the last hour. They held it out. Nia took it with both hands. The grief-speaker did not speak. They had not been introduced and would not be.

Nia ate half the loaf.

She stopped.

She handed the rest back. The grief-speaker wrapped it again and placed it on a small stone plinth set in the corridor wall Nia had not noticed before, which she now realized had been placed there by someone for this purpose. The grief-speaker bowed the small Thren-to-Thren-scale bow the Sixth Current used when a petitioner had eaten correctly. Then they turned and walked down the corridor.

Nia watched them go.

Her stomach woke up.

"How are you," Dhillon said.

"Standing."

"Good. The car is at the east airlock. The First-Speaker has requested you in the lesser chamber at twelve hundred. It is eleven eighteen. You will be a little early."

"All right."

"Are you ready."

"No."

"Good."

He offered his arm. She took it. They walked.

The compound at eleven twenty was on the late-morning cycle, the thin gold light the embassy designers had calibrated for productivity. Nia saw it with the body's particular thin-fast clarity, which was different from the third-interval clarity and less dangerous: it rendered things as themselves, only slightly slowed. She saw Dhillon's coat. She saw Adaeze Okonkwo at the junction, who looked up once, saw her, saw Dhillon, and went back to her slate in a way that meant she would remember the moment. She saw the corridor walls. She saw her own feet.

She did not speak on the walk. Dhillon did not speak.

At eleven forty-two they reached the east airlock. Dhillon released her arm.

"I will be here when you come out."

"All right."

"Nia."

"Yes."

"If the First says no."

"I know what happens."

"All right."

He stepped back. She cycled the airlock.

The lesser chamber was the same chamber it had been two days ago, which was both a relief and a small cruelty, because Nia's body was not the body it had been two days ago. She walked to the tile island. She stood.

The First-Speaker was on the far side, in the same posture of cold listening. The second figure was Vorathan, in attending at an angle, at her left. The third figure, the attendant Nia had not been able to read before, was no longer in the shadow. They were standing at the First-Speaker's right, in a posture Nia thought she now recognized and did not say.

The suspension was warm. The light was the warmer end of the Thren spectrum. Nia's skin rendered in the color of a person who had eaten exactly one meal in the last sixty hours.

The First-Speaker spoke first.

"You have eaten."

"I have."

"You have been heard by the Second Current."

"I have."

"You have been refused by the Fourth and the Third."

"I have."

"You have been consented to by the Sixth."

"Yes."

"That is three Currents of consent and two of refusal."

"Yes."

The First-Speaker was silent for a long moment.

Then she said: "Tell me what you have concluded about the Seventh."

Nia did not pause. She had been carrying the answer for thirty hours, and she had been carrying it in the shape she was about to offer.

"The Seventh Current has not been present at any of the four recorded performances of the mourning rite," she said. "Not as speaker, not as witness, not as listener, not as attendant. Their absence from the record is consistent across two hundred and seventy Thren years. I do not believe their absence is silence. I believe it is a standing posture. In the Thren grammar of presence and absence, a Current that is absent from a rite it has the right to witness is a Current that has declined to hear. Such a Current's absence is itself a communication. I believe the Seventh has, across the history of the rite, communicated the same thing each time: that they do not participate in the rite as other Currents participate, because their participation takes a form the other Currents are not permitted to see. I believe the Seventh has not refused the rite. I believe they have heard every rite from a position the record does not catch."

She stopped.

The First-Speaker did not move.

Then the First-Speaker said: "You have read further than most."

Nia did not answer.

"The Seventh Current sent me word of your hearing at oh seven this morning," the First-Speaker said. "I received it in a register I will not describe to you, and I will not ask you how they came to hear you. The Seventh has granted consent."

Nia did not move for three seconds.

"That is four Currents," the First-Speaker said. "The First Current grants consent. The rite may be opened."

"Thank you."

"I am not finished."

"I apologize."

"You have until the completion of the seventh day of mourning to open the rite. That is one hundred and thirty of your hours from now, approximately four of ours. You will open the rite in the audience chamber where the speaker fell. You will open it as a speaker in the only family you were given, which is the phrase you used on the first day, and which my Current has elected to permit as grounds of standing. You will invite every Thren of the consenting Currents to respond. Any Thren who hears the rite will respond, whether they have been invited or not;

the rite is not an invitation. You will close the rite yourself, in the manner of the closing, which Vorathan has been given permission to teach you in the hours remaining."

She paused.

"You will not survive the rite unaltered. I cannot tell you what will be altered, because I do not know, and because I have never heard of a speaker who could have told anyone in advance. I can only tell you that the speakers who have come out of it have come out of it differently."

"I understand."

"I hope that is true."

"I will close the rite."

"Good."

The First-Speaker closed her three modes in a signature Nia registered as permission-to-proceed, which was not the dismissal-in-formal-register of the first meeting. Vorathan had not spoken throughout. Nia did not look at him. She turned and walked to the airlock and cycled it.

Dhillon was in the corridor.

He looked at her face.

"Yes," she said.

He exhaled once.

"Sixty-odd hours," she said. "A hundred and thirty before the silence ends."

"All right."

"Audience chamber."

"All right."

"Vorathan is to teach me the closing."

"I will arrange it."

She took his arm again, because the sixtieth hour was the sixtieth hour, and she had just agreed to open a rite that would alter her. She walked.

Twenty-Four

Dhillon walked her back to her quarters.

He did not speak on the walk. He did not ask her what was in her head. He made her take his arm a second time when she nearly missed a step at the junction, and he made her sit on the bench in the residential atrium for ninety seconds when her pulse spiked, and he made her drink half a glass of water when she reached her door. He had, in thirty years of civil service, handled more returning-from-Thren-chamber human bodies than Nia wanted to imagine, and he moved around hers with the small practiced courtesies of a man who had done this often enough to know it was the small courtesies that mattered.

At the door he said: "I am going to make three calls."

"All right."

"Vorathan will be permitted to teach you the closing. His Current has agreed. I will confirm the schedule within the hour."

"All right."

"Until then."

"Until then."

He did not wait for her to close the door. He stepped back and turned down the corridor and was gone.

Nia went inside.

She took off her coat. She hung it on the hook. She went into the galley alcove and opened the cooling drawer, which had been restocked overnight by an embassy service she had not requested and had not, at any point in the last three days, remembered existed. Inside were two clear containers labeled in the cautious script of an infirmary dietitian. The first was a thin broth. The second was a small portion of plain steamed rice. A tag on the broth read break with this. A tag on the rice read in forty minutes.

She almost laughed. She almost did not.

She heated the broth. She sat at the counter. She ate it with a spoon, slowly, in the small mouthfuls the tag implied. The broth tasted of salt and of a mineral she could not immediately name and of something faintly green she eventually recognized as Terran parsley, which the embassy botanists kept in a hydroponic tray at the back of the residential kitchen for reasons of morale. The parsley was the morale. She drank half the bowl in eight minutes. She stopped.

She sat with the bowl.

Her stomach did not protest. Her head, which had been thin and spare for thirty-odd hours, began to thicken pleasantly at the edges. She registered the thickening the way she had been trained to register a change in register: with a small note, made silently, for later.

At the forty-minute mark she heated the rice. She ate a third of it. She stopped again.

She did the dishes by hand, because the sonic had been off since she had last been in the kitchen and she did not want the noise.

She undressed in the small bathroom. The clothes she had been wearing for two days came off in the specific stale-cloth way that meant they were going to need to be sent out rather than laundered in the quarters' small unit. She put them in the service bin.

She took a long shower.

The water was hot. She stood under it. She did not hurry. She washed her hair with the small sachet of shampoo the embassy provided in a color she had never identified. She stood with her eyes closed for a long moment near the end and let the water run over the places the fast had thinned: the hollows under her clavicles, the slight hollows at her temples, the hollow at the base of her throat. The water did not fill them. The water reminded her where they were.

She did not look at herself in the mirror. She did not need to. She had eaten. She had eaten twice. Her body knew.

She dried herself. She put on a sleep layer.

She went to the bed.

She lay down.

She did not lie down the way a person lay down after a normal day. She lay down the way a body that had not been in a bed for nearly seventy hours lay down: with relief that felt like a small animal settling. The mattress held her in the specific Concordance-contract way that suggested a medium-firm preference had been marked in her intake forms. The blanket was the blanket. She pulled it up to her collarbone.

She thought, for a moment, about what she was about to carry. She did not think about it long. The sleep was already reaching for her, and she was not going to fight it. She had, for once, nothing she was obligated to do for the next several hours.

She closed her eyes.

She slept.

She slept for eleven hours.

She did not dream. Or she dreamed in the way a body dreams when it has been asked too much and has put the dreaming away for later processing. When she woke it was oh two hundred local in the morning, which the compound was running as the sleep cycle's deepest dark, and she was entirely, startlingly hungry.

She got up.

She ate the rest of the rice. She ate a piece of fruit she found in the cooling drawer she had not noticed earlier, a small apple the embassy greenhouses had coaxed out of a Terran seed stock that had not produced fruit on Sepharu until this year. It tasted like apple. It was, in the compound dark at oh two seventeen, the best thing she had eaten in her adult life.

She drank water. She sat at the counter in the sleep layer with her hair still damp from the shower she had taken before sleeping, and she was alive in the specific way a body is alive after it has been returned to itself. She registered her own pulse. It was back to baseline.

She did not work.

She did not open the terminal.

She did not check the comm.

She went back to the bed.

She slept for another four hours.

When she woke at oh six hundred the simulated sky was shifting toward dawn.

She got up. She ate a small breakfast: toast, a second apple, a cup of tea she made without the pinch of salt Adrian had always put in his. She drank water. She dressed in working clothes, not the suspension layer.

She opened the terminal.

There was a message from Dhillon, sent at twenty-three forty-seven the night before.

Vorathan will be at the east conference room at oh nine. Two hours morning, two hours afternoon, three days. The Fourth Current has permitted this. He cannot teach you in the suspension; he can teach you on paper and in dry air. You will have to practice the three modes alone. I will check on you at midday. The rite opens in a hundred and nineteen hours.

She read the message twice.

She did not close the terminal. Her eye caught on the archive of Vance's private voice memos his staff had forwarded to her after, the ones she had never been able to delete. She chose a file at random. She did not look at the date.

His voice came through quiet, the way he spoke to himself when he thought no one was listening.

"I keep thinking about the quiet places. Not the obvious ones. The other ones. How nobody notices until someone goes there and comes back wrong."

Eleven seconds. No context before or after. The next memo was about a staffing question. The one before had been about a speech on Ganymede. She played the eleven seconds twice. She copied the phrase into the scratch file she kept for things she did not yet know what to do with.

She drank the rest of her water.

She had just over two hours before she needed to be at the east conference room.

She had, when she set the terminal down, a hundred and nineteen hours.

She sat for a minute in the chair at the desk.

Then she stood up and began to prepare.

Twenty-Five

The east conference room was dry.

It was a dry Nia had not registered as dry until she walked into it, because her body had been in the suspension or adjacent to the suspension for so many hours that standard atmosphere now felt like a thinning in the air. The room was a Concordance working space with a long oak-style table, chairs in two rows, a wall screen, and a small kitchenette at the back with a water dispenser and a row of cups upside down on a rack. It was the kind of room in which the Concordance held its internal working sessions. It was not the kind of room in which a Thren had ever, in Nia's memory, been given a chair.

Vorathan was in a chair.

The Fourth Current had sent a piece of their own chamber architecture ahead of him: a small ceremonial cushion set on the seat, which allowed him to sit in the human-scale chair without contorting. He had his forward limbs arranged on the table in the relaxed half-posture of a scholar at work, not the formal posture of attending at an angle. He had a stack of paper in front of him and a pen beside it. The pen had ink in it, which meant he had thought about what he was going to write.

He rose when she came in. She registered the rise as the small Thren-to-human courtesy it was intended as, and she returned it by crossing to him without hesitation and sitting in the chair across.

"Iyana," he said.

"Vorathan."

"Before we begin," he said, "I need to tell you that my Current has not lifted the review. What I am about to teach you, I am teaching with my Current's permission but not with its blessing. If the review goes against me at the end of the seventh day, what I teach you today will be used as evidence. You should know this as you learn it."

"I know it."

"It does not change what I teach."

"I understand."

"Good."

He turned the stack of paper toward her.

"The closing of the rite," he said, "is not one sequence. It is three sequences that have to be performed as one. The trouble for a human speaker is that your body can perform each of the three, but your attention cannot hold all three at once. We will therefore learn them separately and then learn to perform them together. We have twelve hours of teaching. We have three days of your practice. That is enough, if your practice is disciplined."

"It will be."

"I know."

He pointed at the top page. It was covered in a dense Thren notation Nia recognized but had never had cause to read in detail. The notation was three-layered, the way Thren chemistry papers were three-layered when rendered for scholarly work: the first layer for vocalization, the second for pigment, the third for chemical release.

"The first sequence," he said, "is the vocalization. It is three descending tones, each held for a count that corresponds to the number of Currents that have been invited to respond. You have invited six, because the Fifth was not invited. Your count is six. You will hold the first tone for six beats. You will hold the second tone for six beats. You will hold the third tone for six beats. Then you will release. Does your training let you produce the tones?"

"Yes. I can produce them."

"Produce them."

She produced them, in the dry air. Her voice, thinned by the fast and thickened by what she had eaten in its place, carried the three tones at pitches she had practiced in graduate school and had not had occasion to use in the field since. They sounded, in the dry air, smaller than they would sound in the suspension.

Vorathan was silent for a long moment.

"Good," he said. "You have the tones. You will produce them correctly in the suspension, which will catch them and carry them. The second sequence is the pigment-glyph. You will render it on your translator patch. The glyph is this one."

He drew it on the second page, one careful stroke at a time. Nia watched. The glyph was unfamiliar. It was not one of the glyphs her translator patch had been calibrated to carry. Her patch would need to be updated. She noted this and would tell Dhillon.

They worked for forty minutes on the glyph. Vorathan drew it. Nia copied it. Vorathan corrected. Nia copied again. He did not comment when her hand shook on the third copy, because her hand had shaken on the first and second copies as well, and there was no point in naming it.

At the forty-minute mark he sat back and drank from his cup of water, which was, Nia had only now registered, adapted for the shape of a Thren mouth.

"Iyana," he said.

"Yes."

"The young Thren who came to your quarters during the third interval."

She looked up.

"The Seventh did send me word of my hearing," she said, slowly. "The First-Speaker told me so."

"Yes."

"I still do not know whether the visit was real."

"I know."

"Will you tell me."

Vorathan was quiet for a moment.

"I will tell you what I can tell you," he said. "The Seventh does not have a protocol for visiting another Current's petitioner. The Seventh does not send delegates. The Seventh does not appear where they can be seen, because the Seventh has been, since before the Thren had a written language, the Current that represents the part of speech that happens in the absence of a speaker. That is the part I can say clearly. The rest of it I cannot say even to you, because my own Current does not know whether I know it, and I prefer that they continue not to know."

"You are telling me you cannot tell me."

"I am telling you that if someone came to your quarters during the third interval, and if they were the Seventh, they came in a mode I am not permitted to describe. I am also telling you that if no one came to your quarters, and if you hallucinated the visit, that would be a thing the Seventh is known to make possible for a petitioner who has asked the right question in the right register. I do not know which happened. I am not sure any Thren scholar of my standing could know."

"So I speak without knowing."

"You have been speaking without knowing for ten days. Another few hours will not break you."

He returned to the page.

"The third sequence is the chemical release. It is the most dangerous of the three. In the suspension, the rite's compulsion has by the time of the closing filled the volume with response signatures from every speaker who has answered. Those signatures are still active. The closing's chemical sequence neutralizes them. If the sequence is performed correctly, the volume returns to ordinary time. If the sequence is performed incorrectly, the signatures continue to compel response, and the compulsion will find the performer, because the performer is the only being in the chamber who is required by the rite's grammar to keep speaking."

"It would find me."

"It would find you first. Then everyone else."

"How do I perform it correctly."

"You release two signatures in sequence. The first signature is a suppressor, which dampens the active response signatures without erasing them. The second signature is a closing-glyph, which the Thren call the held name: the chemical equivalent of a period at the end of a sentence. Together, they end the rite."

"I do not have either signature in my vials."

"You will have them. I have synthesized them for you. The Fourth Current has permitted me to hand them to you at the door at the end of the third teaching day, in a pair of glass vials prepared to the same specification as your own. Do not open them until you are in the chamber."

Nia did not answer for a long moment.

"You are giving me the things that will save me."

"Yes."

"Your Current will see the record of that."

"Yes."

"Vorathan."

"Do not ask me to stop."

"All right."

He returned to the page. He drew the two signatures in his dense three-layer notation, one above the other, and she copied them, and they continued.

At eleven hundred the morning session ended. Vorathan set his pen down. He did not leave immediately. He sat for a moment in the chair that was not made for him, on the cushion his Current had sent, and he looked at the glyphs on the page between them.

"You will come back at fourteen hundred," he said.

"I will."

"Iyana."

"Yes."

"Eat before you come back."

"I will."

"Good."

She gathered the pages he had given her. She stood. She left the east conference room. She walked back through the corridors to her quarters, and she did not cry, because she was not a person who cried at the memory of a friend drawing two vial-signatures on a page for her, but she felt something sit inside her chest she did not yet have a name for.

She had, when she closed her quarters' door, a hundred and fourteen hours.

Twenty-Six

By the second morning of teaching she could produce each of the three modes cleanly.

She had practiced the tones in her quarters at oh five hundred, oh five thirty, oh six, and oh seven the morning before. She had practiced the pigment-glyph with the calibration update Dhillon had arranged, which had taken a technician three hours, which Nia had not thanked the technician for because she had not been able to find words that would carry. She had practiced the chemical release only in the dry air, without vials, which meant she had practiced the gesture without the content, and the gesture was, in isolation, simple. Each mode alone was something she could do.

She could not do them at once.

She walked to the east conference room at oh eight fifty-seven. Vorathan was already there, in the same chair, on the same cushion, with a different stack of paper. He looked up when she came in. He did not greet her. It was the second morning. They had stopped greeting each other.

"I cannot hold all three," she said, without sitting.

"I know."

"I have been practicing."

"I know."

"The tones go. I lose the glyph halfway through. If I hold the glyph, the chemical timing drifts. If I hold the chemical timing, the tones get flat."

"Sit."

She sat.

"The Thren body," Vorathan said, "carries the three modes as a single grammar. We do not perform them together. We perform them. There is no plural. When a human asks me how I speak, I tell them I do the three things at once, because that is the grammar of your language, and it is not wrong, but it is not the inside of the experience. The inside is that what you are calling three things is one thing. A Thren who has to think about the three modes as three has been badly trained."

He was quiet for a moment. Then he added, more to himself than to her: "My clutch-sibling Oravathen-of-the-Narrow-Count used to say the three modes were three stones carried in one hand. I did not understand the teaching when they gave it. I did not think to ask them to say it a second way. They are not here for me to ask."

Nia registered the past tense. She registered the name. He had spoken once before, obliquely, of a clutch-sibling lost in the hours after the first-contact incident, without naming her. He had given the name now. She did not interrupt. She did not ask.

"That is not useful to me."

"I know. I am going to say something that is."

"All right."

"You cannot acquire our grammar in three days. You are not going to. You are a speaker of another body, and the other body does the three modes as three. What you can do, and what your training has been accidentally preparing you for without either of us knowing it, is build a scaffolding. You pick one mode as your carrier. You let the other two ride on it. When your carrier is strong, the two on it will be weaker than they should be, but they will be present. Present is enough for the rite. The rite does not need you to be a Thren. It needs you to be the speaker the chamber recognizes."

Nia considered this.

"Which mode do I pick."

"Whichever one your body is best at."

She knew which one her body was best at. She had been a linguist before she had been anything else, and a linguist's trained mode was vocalization. Her voice carried the tones more cleanly than her patch rendered the glyph or than her chemistry-vials released the signature. If she used the voice as the carrier, she could anchor there.

"Vocalization," she said.

"Try."

She tried.

She held the first tone for six beats. She rendered the glyph on her patch, three strokes into the carrier, each stroke landing within the tonal window. She cued her chemical release on the count of the fourth beat, which was when Vorathan had shown her the closing needed it. The chemical release, in practice, was only a gesture, a fingers-at-the-vial motion without opening the vial. Her fingers went to the wrong pocket. She lost the beat. The tone thinned. The glyph began to smear on the patch, because the patch was calibrated to the tonal window and her voice had broken out of it.

She stopped.

"Again," Vorathan said.

She tried again.

She lost the glyph at the second tone.

She tried again.

She lost the chemical timing at the third tone.

She tried again.

She held everything, and the third tone came out of her throat as a breath rather than a sound, because her body had spent the tonal air on the first two.

She stopped. She set her hands on the table. She looked at the paper. She did not speak for about twelve seconds.

Then she said, quietly: "I am going to fail in the chamber."

Vorathan did not respond for a moment.

Then he said: "You are not going to fail in the chamber. You are going to fail in this room. That is what this room is for. The chamber is what the next four days are for. Right now you are practicing the failure. The failure is acceptable. What you are doing is useful."

"It does not feel useful."

"It is not supposed to feel useful. If it felt useful, you would not be learning. Feeling useful during practice is a symptom of overfamiliar material. Your material is not overfamiliar. It is the opposite of overfamiliar. It is a Thren rite being taught to a human body for the fifth time in the recorded history of this contact. You are allowed to fail."

Nia did not answer.

"Do it again," Vorathan said.

She did it again.

She did it again after that.

At the eleventh attempt she held all three modes through the first tone, the first glyph-stroke, and the first chemical beat. She lost the second tone. She was closer than she had been.

At the fourteenth attempt she held all three modes through the second tone. She lost the third.

At the seventeenth attempt she held all three modes all the way through.

Her body was shaking by the end. Her voice was thin. The last chemical beat had come three-tenths of a second late. She had held it.

"Again," Vorathan said.

She did it again. She failed. She did it again. She failed differently. At the twenty-first attempt she held it.

"Twice in ten tries," Vorathan said.

"Yes."

"In the chamber you have one attempt."

"I know."

"You will practice this afternoon without me. You will practice tomorrow without me. You will practice the morning of the rite without me. By the time you enter the chamber, two in ten will be seven in ten, and seven in ten is the number a Thren scholar of my standing would accept for a student of mine in the third year. You are not my student and you are not in the third year. Seven in ten is what I am asking for."

"Seven in ten."

"You can do it."

"I hope so."

"I know you can."

Nia looked up at him.

"You do not know that," she said.

"I know that I am telling you that, which is different."

She worked with him until eleven hundred. They did not speak again until the session ended. She held the three modes five more times in twenty-three more attempts, which was two in ten again plus one, which was statistically improvement even if it did not feel like it.

At eleven hundred Vorathan set his pen down. He did not rise this time. He waited for her to gather the pages.

"Iyana," he said.

"Yes."

"Fourteen hundred."

"I will be here."

"Eat first."

"I will."

She gathered the pages. She stood. She left the conference room.

She walked back to her quarters in the compound's late-morning light.

She had, when she closed her door, ninety hours.

She opened the pages. She found her place in the notation. She began to practice.

Twenty-Seven

By the afternoon of the third day she was at seven in ten.

She had reached it at oh eight oh four that morning, without Vorathan, in her quarters. She had reached it again at oh nine forty. She had reached it four more times before the ten hundred session, and a seventh time during the ten hundred session, when Vorathan had asked her to perform the closing cold with no warm-up. The seventh success had arrived dry and slow. It had very nearly not been a success. But it had been a success, and Vorathan had registered it with a small pulse of his signature Nia had come to recognize as something close to a nod.

Seven in ten was the number Vorathan had asked for. Seven in ten had arrived.

She did not trust it.

At fourteen hundred she walked to the east conference room with the fourth and final pair of practice pages folded in her inside coat pocket. The pocket was the same pocket she had used for her own vials, which she had, at Vorathan's instruction, not carried today. Today she was to receive the two he had synthesized for her, and she was to carry them in a pocket prepared for nothing else.

Vorathan was in the conference room when she arrived.

He was not on his cushion. He was standing. He was holding a small lacquered case she had not seen before. His signature was very quiet.

"Iyana," he said.

"Vorathan."

"I have two hours. They are my last two hours. I would like to use them for three things."

"All right."

"The first is to watch you perform the closing three times. If you perform it cleanly, I will give you the vials. If you do not, I will give them to you at the end, and we will use the remainder for correction."

"All right."

"The second is to tell you what I cannot teach."

"All right."

"The third is to say something I need to say while I am still permitted to."

Nia did not answer.

"Let us begin," he said.

She performed the closing.

She performed it cleanly.

She performed it a second time, also cleanly, which she did not allow herself to register as confidence.

She performed it a third time. She lost the glyph at the second tone. She stopped. She did not swear, because she did not swear in the conference room even now. She looked at Vorathan.

"Once more," he said.

She performed it once more.

It was clean.

Vorathan did not speak for a long moment. He set the lacquered case on the table and opened it.

Inside were two glass vials, identical in form to Nia's own: clear, slim, capped in a narrow stopper the Thren used for long-stable compounds. The first was faintly gold. The second was a dark, quiet color Nia could not immediately identify and eventually recognized as the specific indigo of a Thren mantle at rest, a color the Thren almost never synthesized because the Thren almost never needed to.

"The gold is the suppressor," Vorathan said. "The indigo is the held name. Release the gold first. Count three of your beats. Release the indigo. Do not open either until you are standing on the tile island of the audience chamber."

"I won't."

He did not close the case immediately. He set the stoppered gold vial upright in its velvet groove and tapped its crown twice, very lightly, with the side of his thumb. Then he reset the indigo in the same way, twice. Nia registered the gesture as a small private ritual. She did not ask what it was.

He closed the case. He held it out. She took it with both hands.

"What I cannot teach," he said.

"Yes."

"The rite, as you will perform it, will take between eleven and fourteen of your minutes to reach its answering register. During that time, every Thren in the chamber will be compelled to respond in a sequence I have not described to you, because the sequence is not uniform across the Currents. The Thren who responds will know, in the responding, something about herself she may not have known before. This is a thing the rite does. I cannot teach you to expect it, because I cannot predict it. I can only tell you that when it happens, you will be the only speaker in the chamber who is not responding. You will be speaking. Every other speaker will be answering you."

"All right."

"You will feel the responses as a kind of heat along your skin. It is not heat. It is the chemistry of the responses settling against your body because your body is the focus of the rite. The Thren literature calls it the wearing. It is the thing that has killed two of the four performers in the history of the rite, though none of them was human."

"I understand."

"You will not understand until you feel it. I am telling you so that when you feel it, you do not mistake it for something you are doing wrong. You will not be doing anything wrong. The wearing is the rite doing what it does."

"All right."

"Do not stop because of the wearing. Do not stop for any reason. If you stop, the chamber will not forgive it. You will have to open the rite a second time. You will not have the strength or the consent to do so."

"I won't stop."

"Good."

He was silent for a moment.

Then he said: "The third thing."

"Yes."

"My Current will decide my review at the completion of the seventh day of mourning. That is fourteen hours after the rite, which means that if you open the rite at the beginning of the final day, my Current will decide my review while you are still in the chamber answering your own rite. I will not be in the chamber with you. I am not of your family and not of your Current, and the rite does not permit me in any register. I have been told, as a matter of courtesy, where the Current will sit during my review. They will sit in the scholars' range, in the chair Nemari held when she refused you."

"Vorathan."

"I am not telling you this because I want you to carry it into the chamber. I am telling you because I want you to know that if you do not see me again after today, it will not be because the Current decided against you. It will be because the Current decided against me. That is a distinction I want you to hold."

"Yes."

"I do not believe they will decide against me. I am telling you this anyway, because a Thren of my Current does not leave a petitioner he has trained without naming what is possible."

"I understand."

"Good."

She did not cry. She did not reach across the table. She did not move. The lacquered case was in her hands. The glyphs he had drawn over three days were folded in her inside pocket. The two vials in the case were warmer than the conference room air, because he had carried them against his body until she arrived.

"Vorathan," she said.

"Yes."

"Thank you for the vials."

"That is not what you meant to say."

"No."

"Say it."

She did not say it. Her throat had thinned in the way it had thinned on the ninth day, and she did not trust what would come out of it. She set the lacquered case against her chest with both hands.

He understood.

He rose.

"I will see you after," he said.

"Yes."

"If I do not."

"I know."

He cycled his three modes into a small signature Nia had never read in the field and had not expected to feel. It was not a goodbye signature. It was a signature the Thren used between speakers who had been through a rite together, and were agreeing, without saying so, to that fact. Nia had read about it in one footnote of one monograph. She had not expected to be on the receiving end of it.

He turned. He left the conference room.

She sat alone with the lacquered case.

She sat for a long time.

Then she stood. She walked to her quarters. She did not practice for the rest of the day. She drank water. She ate a small meal. She lay down on the bed in the late afternoon and she rested without sleeping.

She had, when she closed her eyes, seventy-two hours.

Three of her days. Three of them.

She had learned what she could learn.

She waited.

Twenty-Eight

She lay on the bed without sleeping for nearly an hour.

The lacquered case was on her chest. She had taken it there when she had lain down, because she had not wanted to set it on the bedside table and look at it from across the room, and because she had not been able to put it in the drawer with her own vials, which would have meant opening the drawer, which would have meant a gesture. She had not been up to a gesture. So she had lain down on her back with the case against her sternum and her hands loose at her sides. She had closed her eyes. She had not slept.

The case was warm.

She registered the warmth at seventeen forty-three. She had registered it when she had taken it from Vorathan's hands. She had remarked on it, silently, to herself, with the particular kind of noticing she reserved for details that carried more than their weight. She had not let herself register what the warmth meant.

The warmth was Vorathan's body.

He had carried the case against his chest in the hour before he had given it to her, so the vials would not be cold to her hand when he passed them. She had been warm on his chest. She was cold on hers. The case was still warm because it had only been an hour.

It would not be warm in the morning.

She began to cry.

She cried the way a person cries when she has not given herself permission and the permission has arrived anyway, which was to say silently, without thrashing, with her face wet, her breath held, and her hands still loose at her sides. She cried for Vorathan.

She cried for Vorathan because the Fourth Current was going to decide his review while she was in the chamber answering her rite. She cried because he had drawn the closing-signatures for her in his own hand over three days, when his Current was measuring how much he was willing to compromise his standing for her. She cried because he had used her first name twice, and because his name for her had been a gift she had not known how to receive. She cried because he would not be in the chamber with her and might never be in a room with her again. She cried because he had called her Iyana. She cried because the case on her chest was the warmth of his body, and the warmth was leaving.

She did not cry long for Vorathan. She cried enough.

Then she cried for Adrian.

She cried for Adrian differently. The grief for Vorathan had been a grief in which she could name who was dying, which was possibly her. The grief for Adrian was a grief in which she could not name what had died, because the thing that had died had happened before she had met him, in a calculation someone had made about who could be compromised and how.

She cried for the afternoon in the compound garden on day five, when he had walked beside her on the Terran grass under the sun lamp and had talked about a paper he had read recently, which she now knew had been a paper that documented the technology that would kill Vance three days later. She cried for the tea he had always made with a pinch of salt. She cried for the hand he had placed around her wrist the first night, which she had let him place there because he had been the person in the room who had been, for the length of time it took the tea to cool, a friend.

She cried for their years at the academy, when she had been twenty-four and he had been thirty. She had believed the problem between them was distance. The problem had never been distance.

She cried for the fact that he had come to her quarters with his own slate and had held himself too carefully. He had been holding himself too carefully because he had already agreed to kill the man standing beside her.

She cried for him because he was going to be in the chamber on the other side of her rite, and she was going to find him there. The rite found what it was called to find. She had called it to find him.

Then she cried for herself.

The tears did not come as easily for herself. She had been trained, by a mother who had been trained by a Nigerian grandmother who had been trained by someone else, that one did not cry first for oneself. She cried for herself third, because that was the register her family had given her, and she did not cry long.

She cried for her own body. She cried for the body the rite would wear. Vorathan had told her it had killed two of the four performers, and none of them had been human, and she understood what that meant without having the training to believe she understood. She cried for her hands, which had been trained to notation since she had been seven and which might stop working in the chamber if the wearing reached her hands first. She cried for her voice, which she needed for the tones, and which she might not have when she needed it. She cried for the simple fact that she would prefer to live, which she had not admitted to herself, because admitting it would have been a softness she had not been able to afford.

She did not cry long for herself. She cried enough.

Then she sat up.

She sat up on the bed with her hair in a mess and her face wet and the lacquered case in her lap. She looked at the simulated sky, which was beginning its evening shift at seventeen fifty-one in the compound's calibration. She did not wipe her face. She did not apologize to the case. She was past those courtesies now.

She understood what she had been refusing to understand.

There was no one else who could do this.

She had been carrying that fact for three days, since the First-Speaker had granted consent. She had not let herself carry it as a fact. She had carried it as a problem to be solved. The problem had been solved. The four Currents had consented. The closing had been taught. The vials were in her lap. The fact of the matter was that the person who was going to walk into the chamber in seventy-one hours was her, and no one else, because no one else had been standing at Vance's right hand side when he fell, and no one else had read what had killed him in real time, and no one else had stayed awake at her desk for the night Adrian had pinged her comm twice, and no one else had been the person the First-Speaker had indulged, and no one else had been taught the closing by a Fourth Current scholar willing to lose his standing to teach it.

She was the speaker.

She had been the speaker since the ninth day.

She wiped her face with the back of her hand. She was done.

She set the lacquered case on the bedside table. She stood up. She went into the small bathroom and washed her face. She did not look at herself in the mirror again, because she did not need to. She had eaten. She had slept. She had cried. Her body knew.

She came back to the bed.

She put her hand on the case.

It was still warm.

It would be cool by morning. It would be cool when she opened it in the chamber.

She would be the warmth in the chamber. The vials would have her warmth in them when she released them, because she would have carried them against her chest the way Vorathan had carried them against his, and what the rite would find would be a signature she had warmed into being.

She understood this. She had understood it since he had given her the case. She had been refusing to understand it, because understanding it had required her to feel what she had just felt.

She had felt it.

She was ready.

She lay down again.

She slept this time.

She slept for eleven hours, which was more than she had expected. She slept with the lacquered case on the bedside table at her shoulder, and she did not dream of the chamber.

When she woke it was oh five hundred local, and she had, according to the terminal clock, sixty-one hours.

She did not count.

She had learned what she could learn. She had grieved what she could grieve. The work that remained was practice and preparation. She had three days of it. She did not need to count the hours.

She got up.

She put on working clothes.

She went to practice.

Twenty-Nine

On the first morning of practice she reached nine in ten by eleven hundred.

She had started at oh six, because her body had decided, on waking after the long sleep, that it was ready to work. She had run the three modes separately first, which was the discipline Vorathan had taught her on the second day: warm the tones, warm the glyph, warm the chemical gesture without the vials, and then bring them together. She had held seven of the first ten. She had held eight of the next ten. She had held nine of the ten after that.

She did not celebrate. Seven in ten on Vorathan's last teaching day had been seven in ten with Vorathan in the chair across. Nine in ten alone in her quarters was not the same thing.

She practiced another thirty attempts before she ate.

The first full practice day had a rhythm she did not design and did not resist.

She practiced at oh six, at oh nine, at eleven. She ate at twelve. She practiced at fourteen, at fifteen-thirty, at seventeen. She ate at nineteen. She walked for twenty minutes around the residential corridor, which was permitted now that her confinement had been unofficially eased following the First Current's consent. No escort followed her. She returned to her quarters at twenty. She practiced once more, slowly, at twenty-one. She went to bed at twenty-two.

She slept for seven hours. She dreamed of chamber geometry in a way her body would not remember on waking.

Dhillon's message came on the morning of the second practice day, at oh seven fourteen. She had been eating toast.

It said the invitation list was final, that he had sent the formal invitations to the human attendees in a cover register he would brief her on when she came by the civil service wing, and that the Thren side of the invitation had been handled by the First-Speaker's office, with the Concordance signaling only its human attendance. He had invited fourteen humans. He named them at the bottom of the message.

Nia read the list.

The Concordance senior staff on the delegation: seven names. The Concordance embassy senior clerical staff: three names. A Concordance xenobiologist she had not met. Ilsia Moreau. Two names from the research wing, one of whom was Halpern-Ødegård.

And, at the bottom, as if it were an unremarkable line item in an administrative list: Dr. Adrian Cho.

She read the other names once more. Seven senior delegation staff, three senior clerks, the xenobiologist she had never met, Ilsia Moreau, the two research-wing names, and Adrian. Fourteen humans. She had an attendance for every human who had been in the ninth-day chamber and every human who had touched the falsified chemistry in the days after, and she had them all on one list, with Adrian's name at the bottom, where Dhillon had placed it not for emphasis but because that was where an Adrian Cho alphabetically landed when Dr. Tamar Halpern-Ødegård was three names above him.

She set the toast down.

She read the list a second time. She read it slowly.

She had known Adrian was going to be on the list. That was the whole of it. The list existed in order to have Adrian on it. The fact of seeing his name printed in ordinary civil service formatting, in a paragraph that also contained Halpern-Ødegård's name, was nevertheless a small precise blow, and she registered it as one.

She wrote back to Dhillon: I am coming by.

She walked to the civil service wing at oh eight hundred.

Dhillon was at his desk in the inner office, with the door open. The legal counsel woman was not in the outer room. The man in charcoal was not in the outer room. Dhillon stood when Nia came in.

"Doctor."

"Dhillon."

"You saw the list."

"I saw the list."

"The cover register is the Thren apology rite."

"Yes."

"The humans were invited in those terms. The Thren side was not told the cover register, because they do not need it; they know what the rite is. The cover is for us. The cover is also, incidentally, true. The rite does include an apology, in the Thren reading of it. The rite apologizes to the chamber."

"I did not know that."

"The Thren called it the apology to the volume. It is not a phrase we translate often. It is not a phrase the Thren use to us often."

"The humans will believe the cover."

"Yes."

"And you have told the humans that attendance is expected."

"I have told them attendance is an expression of support for the peace, which is the language Concordance senior staff understand as mandatory."

"Adrian."

"Adrian replied within an hour. He will attend."

Nia nodded.

She did not ask how Dhillon had phrased the invitation to Halpern-Ødegård. She did not need to know.

"Thank you," she said.

"Doctor."

"Yes."

"He will come by your quarters."

"I know."

"I am not telling you because I think you do not know. I am telling you because you should be ready for it."

"I will be ready."

"Good."

She walked back through the compound to her quarters.

She did not practice for an hour. She sat at the desk. She watched the simulated sky run through the late-morning cycle, which on this compound was calibrated to suggest a Northern Hemisphere autumn, which Nia had always found slightly off and had never objected to.

She thought about what she would say to Adrian.

She did not think long.

She had been thinking about it for four days without letting herself think about it, which was the kind of thinking that did not require writing down, because the shape of it had been assembling itself in the parts of her mind that assembled shapes without supervision. What she would say when he came was going to be a small lie told with sad practical care. The lie had been in her since the first night. It had been refining itself since the second. She did not need to rehearse it now.

She practiced the closing instead.

She held it eight of ten.

The afternoon passed.

She practiced. She ate. She walked a second twenty minutes. She did not message Ilsia, who she now registered as a person she was going to have to manage after the rite, if she survived it. She did not message Adrian, who she was going to manage today. She was, she registered with a small specific professional satisfaction, entering the last day before the rite in a state she could use.

At seventeen twenty-three there was a knock at her door.

She knew the knock. She had heard it twice in the last ten days. It was Adrian's.

She stood up.

She went to the door.

Thirty

Adrian was in the corridor.

He was not in his delegation coat. He was in a sweater she had not seen him wear on Sepharu, which was not new but was clean, and which she registered with the specific distance of a linguist reading a register choice. The sweater was the sweater he wore when he wanted to be approached. He had put it on before coming. She registered, too, without attaching a meaning to it, a small pale square at the hinge of his jaw below his left ear, of the sort the infirmary used for slow-release patches. She filed the detail the way she had been filing most things in the last ten days: with a tag and no context.

"Nee," he said.

"Adrian."

"Can I come in."

"Yes."

He stepped past her into her quarters and she closed the door behind him. The door clicked. She did not lock it, because she did not need to, because the only person who was going to come to her tonight was already in the room.

He stood for a moment, looking at the quarters. The lacquered case was not visible; she had put it in the drawer with her own vials that morning. The practice pages were on the desk. Adrian's eye moved across the desk and lingered for less than a second on the pages, and then moved on.

"You look good," he said.

"I look terrible."

"You look like a person who has been through something and is still standing. That is what good looks like. I have been a man in this compound for a while."

"Sit."

He sat in the chair by the window. She sat on the couch, opposite him, at the angle where they had sat the first night. She did not sit close. He registered this and did not close the distance.

"I brought you something."

He set a small package on the low table between them. It was wrapped in the sort of paper the embassy commissary sold for small gifts, tied with a cord.

"Tea," he said. "The kind you liked. I had Earth send it on the last supply gate. I ordered it three weeks ago."

"Three weeks ago."

"Yes."

"Before."

"Yes."

She looked at the package. She did not pick it up. She did not thank him for it.

"How are you," he said.

"Standing."

"Dhillon told me you were fasting."

"I was. I finished three days ago."

"The Sixth Current brought you the bread."

"Yes."

"I have never seen that."

"No."

"Are you eating."

"Yes."

"Sleeping."

"Yes."

He nodded. He did not ask more. He had always known, in a way that had been part of what she had loved at twenty-four, how to read a brevity.

"I got the invitation," he said.

"I know."

"It said the rite was an apology."

"It is."

Nia did not pause. She had been refining this for four days, and she had refined it specifically for the moment in which he would ask.

"The Thren call it an apology to the volume," she said. "In their reading of the rite, the chamber itself has been violated by the speech that killed Vance, by the collapse of the ceremony, by the withdrawal of the Currents. The chamber, in the Thren grammar, is a participant in any ceremony conducted inside it. The rite apologizes to the chamber. It restores the ceremonial integrity that was broken on the ninth day. Every Thren of the four consenting Currents will be present. The Concordance was invited to send witnesses. Dhillon told the humans it was a gesture of support for the peace, which is the part you heard, which is also true. Both readings are true. That is how Thren ceremonies are."

Adrian listened.

She did not elaborate. She had been taught in her first year of graduate school that a good lie told with a true explanation at its side was heard by the listener as a single true statement, and that the explanation did not need to make the lie larger. She had made her lie small. She had given him the apology to the volume, which was true. She had not mentioned what the rite would find.

"It sounds important," Adrian said.

"It is."

"You are opening it."

"I am."

"Nee."

"Yes."

"Why you."

"Because I was standing next to Vance when he fell. The First-Speaker allowed the rite on those grounds. A Thren of any Current requires a family-level speaker to open the rite, and I had a claim to that standing by being the speaker at the foot of the dying body. It is a thin grounds. The First-Speaker accepted it. She accepted me as a speaker in the only family I was given. She did not accept other Concordance staff. I am the only human she would allow into the chamber for this."

"That is a reason."

"Yes."

"That is not the whole reason."

"No."

"Will you tell me the rest."

"Not today."

"All right."

He sat back in the chair. He looked at her for a long moment.

"I am not sure I should come," he said.

Nia did not pause.

"You have to come."

"Nee, listen."

"No. Listen. I do not want to explain this. I want you to come. If you do not come, the rite will be incomplete. I will have to do it twice. The First-Speaker will allow me to do it twice on technical grounds, and she will allow it because she indulges me, but she will not forgive me for making her do it. The Fourth Current will read it as weakness. I will lose Vorathan in a way I will not survive."

"Vorathan."

"Yes."

"He is important to you."

"He is important to the rite. He taught me the closing. His Current is going to decide his standing during the rite itself, which is a thing that has only been possible to them because my rite is happening. If the rite is incomplete, he loses. I need you to come."

Adrian looked at her.

She had not planned the Vorathan line. She had planned an appeal to his sense of decency. The Vorathan line had come out because she was tired and it was true, in the narrow sense that Vorathan's standing was tied to the rite completing. She let it stand. It was working in a way the decency appeal would not have worked.

"All right," he said.

"Promise me."

"Nee."

"Promise me."

He stood up. She stood up. He crossed to her, and he put his arms around her the way he had learned to do at twenty-four, right arm across her shoulders, left at her lower back, and he held her.

She held him back.

She kissed him on the mouth.

"Come to the rite," she said against his mouth.

"I will come."

"Promise me."

"I promise, Nee."

"Good."

She pulled back, but she did not step away. She kept her hand on the side of his face for a count of two. He did not move. He did not say anything. He was holding himself as still as he had held himself the first night, which was the stillness she had read on him twice in her life and had now read on him a third time, which she had been careful not to register while she kissed him and which she registered now.

She stepped back.

He stood for a moment with his arms empty.

Then he picked up his coat.

He went to the door.

He paused with his hand on the frame.

"I will see you at the rite," he said.

"Yes."

"Nee."

"Yes."

"I love you."

She did not answer.

He went.

She stood in the quarters for a long moment.

She did not sit down. She walked to the low table. She picked up the package. She unwrapped it. Inside was a small tin of the tea, a dark green compressed leaf of a Nigerian variety her mother had drunk, which she had mentioned to Adrian exactly once in her life, at twenty-four, at a table at the Academy, where Adrian had written it down in his notebook without comment and had never mentioned it to her again. He had remembered. He had ordered it three weeks ago.

She put the tin on the counter in the galley alcove.

She did not open it.

She sat at the desk. She opened her practice pages. She practiced.

She practiced until she could not practice.

She ate a small meal. She drank water. She went to the bed. She lay down with the lacquered case on the bedside table at her shoulder, and she closed her eyes.

Tomorrow was the chamber.

She had, when she slept, fifteen hours.

Thirty-One

She woke at oh five hundred without the alarm.

The compound's simulated sky was still on the sleep cycle's deepest dark, which the designers had calibrated to end at oh five thirty. She had beaten it by half an hour. Her body had decided when to wake. Her body had been deciding a lot of things lately. She did not argue with it.

She lay in the bed for a long minute with her eyes open in the dark. She registered her own pulse. It was slightly high, in the way a pulse went slightly high before a difficult thing. It was within the range she had been trained to expect. She breathed out. She sat up.

She stood.

She went to the bathroom. She used it. She washed her face and her hands and the back of her neck. She did not look in the mirror. She did not need to. She had made her face a year ago and it was the face she had.

She dressed carefully.

She put on the suspension undergarment the embassy issued, which she had laundered and folded the night before. She put on the outer layer with the flared wrists. She put on the pigment-patch, which the technician had recalibrated with Vorathan's new glyph and which she had tested last night against the practice pages and which had held. The patch sat against her sternum the way it had sat against Vance's. She did not linger on the thought.

She did not put on her coat.

She went to the drawer.

She opened it.

She took out the two glass vials of her own remaining notation-signatures and she placed them in the inside left pocket of her outer layer, in the small felt pouch the embassy issued for exactly this purpose. She took out the lacquered case. She opened it. The two vials Vorathan had synthesized for her were still the colors they had been when he handed them to her: the suppressor faintly gold, the held name the dark indigo of a Thren mantle at rest. She placed them in the inside right pocket, which she had chosen specifically because her hand reached it more cleanly under pressure.

She closed the case. She left it on the desk. She would not need it again.

She ate a small breakfast.

She drank tea that was not Adrian's. She had boiled water and dropped in a plain commissary sachet, which tasted of nothing in particular and which she had needed to taste of nothing in particular. She drank the full cup. She drank a glass of water after. She ate a single piece of toast, because the embassy infirmary literature said a single piece of toast was the correct pre-rite fuel for a human body after a broken fast, and Nia had learned over the last ten days to respect the embassy infirmary literature.

At oh seven hundred she practiced the closing one last time, without the vials, in the dry air of her quarters.

She held it.

She did not try again. She did not want to practice a failure into her muscle memory in the last hour.

She sat at the desk for thirty minutes without working. She let the quarters hold her. She let herself be a person sitting in a room who was about to do a thing.

At oh seven forty-four there was a knock.

She knew the knock.

It was Dhillon.

He was in the formal blue-and-grey this morning, which she registered as the correct choice for a man walking a junior linguist to the opening of a Thren rite that was also, to most of the humans present, an apology ceremony. He had dressed for the humans. He had dressed to look like the civil service.

"Doctor."

"Dhillon."

"It is time."

"Yes."

"Do you have what you need."

"Yes."

"Do you need anything else."

"No."

"All right."

He stepped back from the doorway. She put on her coat. She picked up nothing else, because she was carrying everything she needed on her body. She closed her door behind her. She did not lock it.

They walked.

The compound at oh seven fifty on the seventh day of mourning was quiet in a register she had not encountered before. Staff she did not know were in the corridors. They did not speak. They did not step aside; they did not need to, because they had already been somewhere Nia was not, and their paths crossed hers without meeting. The compound was running on the morning cycle, the thin gold light calibrated for productivity, and the productivity it was calibrated for was, today, the productivity of a rite Nia was opening.

Adaeze Okonkwo was at the junction of the residential and civil service wings.

She looked at Nia. Nia looked at her.

Adaeze performed the small service-internal gesture she had performed in the corridor on the day of the brief. The gesture meant, approximately: I see you, I cannot help you, I hope it works.

Nia nodded.

Adaeze bowed her head once, which was not the gesture. The head-bow was Adaeze's own.

Nia walked past her.

They reached the long corridor that led to the audience chamber.

The corridor was full.

The Thren side of the invitation had been arranged by the First-Speaker's office, but the embassy had not expected, and had not been briefed on, the number of Thren who had come to witness. Nia counted seventeen as she walked the corridor, which was every senior scholar of the four consenting Currents and several she did not recognize. They stood along the walls. They did not speak. Their signatures were held so tight she could not read them. She walked past them and did not look directly at any one of them, because she had not been trained in what to do with seventeen Thren senior scholars standing in a single corridor.

The humans were in a cluster near the chamber door. Nia saw them in the shape she had prepared for in her head: fourteen, in delegation-issued suspension layers over their formal attire. Ilsia Moreau was among them. Halpern-Ødegård was among them. Adrian was among them.

Adrian did not look at her.

He was standing at the back of the cluster, in a suit she had not seen him wear, holding his hands folded in front of him the way a man held his hands when he had decided the only thing he was going to do until the ceremony was not move.

She did not look at him either.

Dhillon took her to the air-lock threshold.

He stopped. He turned to face her. He did not offer his arm this time. He knew she had to walk the last few steps alone.

"Doctor."

"Yes."

"I will be in the chamber with you. In the first rank of the human arc."

"I know."

"If I can help."

"You cannot help."

"No."

"I know."

"Good."

He stepped back. The air-lock cycled. The outer door of the audience chamber opened.

Nia looked at it for one beat.

She walked in.

Thirty-Two

The suspension took her at the threshold.

It was warmer than the lesser chamber. It was deeper. It had been charged, Nia registered with a small scholarly note she could not help making, to the specific chemistry the mourning rite required, which was a calibration she had read about in two monographs and had never had occasion to feel. The suspension was dense against her face. The light was the old amber-green the audience chamber ran for full ceremonies. The color was already present, in the sense that the signatures of the assembled Thren were settled into the volume before she had crossed the airlock, and the signatures were arranged around the tile island the way signatures arranged themselves around a speaker.

She walked to the tile island.

The tile island was the same tile island it had been on the ninth day. She had stood on it, beside Vance, in a posture she had held for eight days before the ninth and which she could still feel in her shoulders if she let herself. She had stood on it, and then kneeled, with Vance's head against her thigh. She had stood in front of it, with the suspension draining around her, when they had carried him out.

She stood on it now.

She turned.

The chamber was arranged.

Seventeen Thren of the four consenting Currents were in the upper and middle registers. The First-Speaker was at the far upper tier, in the posture of opened listening, which was the posture the First Current used for a rite it had authorized. The Sixth Current speaker was in the middle tier, in attending-in-grief. The Second Current was in two working alcoves Nia had not known the audience chamber had. The Fourth Current was present, including Nemari-of-the-Long-Reading, who did not look at Nia. Vorathan was not visible. She had been told he would not be. The Seventh was not visible. She had been told they might not be.

The humans were at the far end of the volume, arranged in the lower-tier arc the audience chamber held in its architecture for ceremonies requiring human witness. Fourteen of them, in delegation-issued suspension layers, their pigment-patches carrying the glyph for witness-in-rite. Ilsia Moreau was in the second rank. Halpern-Ødegård was in the first. Adrian was at the back. He was looking at her now. He was not moving.

Dhillon was among them, in the first rank, in his formal blue-and-grey adapted for suspension-entry.

She did not wait.

She lifted her right hand at her side, fingers spread, in the gesture the service had called listening-to-learn ten days ago and which she was using today for a different purpose. The gesture registered in the chamber as the opening signal of a petitioner-in-rite. The Thren in the upper and middle registers cycled their signatures, once, in acknowledgment.

She drew a breath.

She began.

Her vocalization was small and precise. She produced the opening tones, which were not the closing tones she had practiced for a week but the opening tones, which were three ascending rather than three descending, which had been taught to her in her doctoral training as a scholarly exercise and which she had never expected to perform in a chamber. The first tone held for the count of four, which was the count of consenting Currents. The second tone held for four. The third tone held for four.

Her pigment-patch rendered the opening-glyph, which was not the closing glyph Vorathan had taught her but the opening glyph the Concordance had published in a treaty annex twelve years ago and which the embassy patch had been calibrated to carry since the first year of contact.

Her chemical register released, at her throat and at her cuffs, the Thren name of the mourning.

She did not think about the name. She said the name.

The chamber answered.

The First-Speaker's silver-green rose, slow, from the upper tier, and moved across the volume in the pattern Nia had read about and had never seen in the field. The Second Current's tight flat signature pulsed twice and held. The Sixth Current's amber settled against Nia's wrists the way it had settled in the shell chamber. The Fourth Current's indigo held without moving. The First, the Sixth, the Second, the Fourth: each of them acknowledged, in their own register, that the rite was open.

The Seventh did not acknowledge.

Nia did not stop. She had been told the Seventh would not acknowledge. She had been told not to wait for them.

She continued.

The rite moved into its answering register faster than she had been taught to expect, which Vorathan had warned her about in the second teaching day: the rite accelerated in response to a speaker of high focus, and Nia had, by virtue of her linguistic training, more focus than the literature had modeled. The acceleration was a feature. The acceleration was also a cost. She would reach the point of compulsion sooner than the seminar papers predicted.

She registered the acceleration and did not try to slow it.

She moved into the compulsion sequence.

The compulsion sequence was the part of the rite that required every chemically-capable being in the suspension to respond. She had studied it. She had memorized what she was going to say. She had practiced the pacing with Vorathan on the second teaching afternoon, at low volume, in dry air. She had not been able to practice it at full volume because the suspension it required had not existed outside the audience chamber itself.

She was in the suspension now.

She produced the compulsion phrase.

She produced it in all three modes, and she produced it at the full volume of her voice. The pigment-patch rendered its strongest glyph. Her chemical register released the second vial of her own notation, a phrase she had synthesized at twenty-six for a seminar paper and had carried through three planets for this moment, which was the phrase she had come to think of, privately, as the name of a dying speaker.

The compulsion was the word for Vance.

The Thren in the chamber responded.

They responded in a sequence Nia did not control and could not have controlled. The First-Speaker responded first, in a signature Nia registered as the First Current's ritual formula for an answered mourning. The Second Current responded next, their tight flat signature unfolding into the working-witness posture the Second used for decisions of record. The Sixth Current responded third, and their amber warmed and spread through the chamber in a way that made Nia's eyes wet. The Fourth Current responded fourth, their indigo thin and careful, which Nia understood as Nemari granting what Nemari had not granted in the scholars' range.

The Seventh did not respond.

Nia had been told.

She kept going.

She had been in the compulsion for nine minutes when the wearing began.

It began as a warmth along her wrists, which was where the Sixth Current's amber had settled. Then a warmth along her shoulders, which was where the First-Speaker's silver-green rested. Then a warmth along her sternum, which was where the Second Current's tight flat had drifted. The warmths were not unpleasant. They were the chemistry of the responses settling against her skin because her body was the focus of the rite. Vorathan had told her she would register them as heat. They registered as heat.

She kept speaking.

She held the three modes. She held the carrier. She let the other two ride it. The scaffold held.

The humans were watching.

Adrian was looking at her.

The compulsion had not reached him yet.

Thirty-Three

The wearing deepened.

It was along her throat now, and along the underside of her jaw, and along the bones of her wrists where the Sixth Current's amber had settled first. It was heavier than the seminar literature had described. She had been in the compulsion for eleven minutes. The rite had been taught to her to last between eleven and fourteen. She was at the threshold of the answering register. The chamber was full of settled responses from the four consenting Currents, each one pressing against her skin the way Vorathan had warned her it would.

She kept speaking. She kept the carrier. She held the closing-glyph in her awareness as a pattern she would render when the answering was complete.

The answering was not complete yet.

The chamber waited.

Nia was aware of her own hands in a way she had not been a minute earlier. The fast had thinned her hands. The wearing was thickening them. She registered both sensations without allowing either one to move her attention from the carrier. The voice was where she lived now. The voice was going to carry the last of it.

She moved into the final register of the compulsion.

In the suspension at the far end of the volume, the humans had been standing in their delegation-issued suspension layers, not moving. Fourteen of them. Adrian at the back. Halpern-Ødegård three positions forward.

The rite, in its accelerating answering register, had not required them to respond. They were humans. They were not chemically-capable in the register the rite compelled. They had been admitted as witnesses.

Nia knew this.

She had also been told by Vorathan, in the third and final teaching session, that the rite compelled every chemically-capable being in the suspension, not every biologically chemical being. The distinction was a Thren distinction. A chemically-capable being was any being whose chemistry was legible to the rite's grammar. A human was not, in general, legible. A human carrying a device calibrated to produce Thren-legible chemistry was.

Adrian was carrying such a device.

She did not know how she knew.

She had, by the eleventh minute of the compulsion, begun to know things the rite wanted her to know.

The compulsion reached him at the twelfth minute.

It did not reach him as it had reached the Currents. It reached him as a small specific pressure at the center of his chest, where the device he had carried into the chamber was set. The device was not a Concordance-issued instrument. It was the device he had used on the ninth day. It had been permitted into the chamber this morning because he had believed, and the civil service had not argued, that a scholar of his standing would carry no instrument into an apology rite.

The device had been set to suppress.

The compulsion was stronger than the suppression.

Nia watched the device fail.

She watched it in the chemistry before she saw it with her eyes. The color in the upper volume of the chamber, above and behind the human arc, began to bloom in a pattern Nia recognized on first sight, because she had spent the last ten days memorizing the pattern, because the pattern was the pattern of the poison that had killed Vance, because the device was producing the exact synthetic signature it had produced on the ninth day.

The signature was small.

The signature was unmistakable.

The Thren in the chamber saw it. Every Thren of the four consenting Currents saw it, because every Thren was trained to read chemistry at the level the rite was operating at, because the rite had called their attention to exactly this register. Their signatures turned, as one, toward the upper volume above the human arc.

The First-Speaker's silver-green moved across the volume slowly.

The Sixth Current's amber coiled.

The Fourth Current's indigo held.

The Second Current's tight flat registered the evidence and entered it into their working record.

Adrian's body reacted to the compulsion the way any body reacted to a chemical signal forced out of itself against its own will. He did not step forward. He did not move his hands. His face did not change. But his signature, which was the signature his device had been suppressing for ten days, was now in the volume of the chamber, visible to every Thren who knew what to look for. He had become, in the chemistry of the chamber, legible.

He had been the one standing closest to the upper volume on the ninth day.

He was the one standing closest to it now.

The weight of the chamber shifted. Nia felt it across her shoulders, across her jaw, along the underside of her tongue. The responses that had been pressing against her skin now carried, underneath them, the small hard fact of the synthetic signature, which the chamber had received as a new answer from a speaker it had not, until this moment, understood to be a speaker. The Thren register for the recognition was not in any human notation. Nia registered it anyway.

The humans did not, at first, understand what had happened. They were not trained in Thren chemistry. They saw a color in the upper volume and they saw the Thren all turning, and they understood there was a thing.

Halpern-Ødegård understood first. Her face, which had been arranged in the careful neutral of a scholar attending a ceremony, changed in a way Nia registered at the level of peripheral attention, because Nia was in the answering register of the rite and was holding the three modes and had almost nothing left for peripheral attention but had this.

Halpern-Ødegård looked at Adrian.

Dhillon, in the first rank of the human arc, looked at Adrian.

Adrian looked at Nia.

He looked at her.

The chamber held still. The Thren did not move. The humans in the arc were turning now, the ones with the training to read the color-map, looking between Adrian and the upper volume and back to Adrian. The suspension was as quiet as Nia had ever stood in. The answering register had gone past its peak and was, in its own slow way, beginning to recede. She was still speaking. She had not stopped. She had been told not to stop.

His face was the face she had known since she was twenty-four, which had sat across from her at the academy table, which had slept on the pillow beside her for two years of her life, which had been in her quarters on the first night of Vance's death with his hand around her wrist.

His face was the face that had kissed her last night, in her quarters, against the promise he had made. His face was the face of a man who had understood, in the fraction of a second between his device's failure and her turning toward him, that she had known, and that the rite she had invited him to was the rite that had found him, and that the hug and the kiss had been the hug and the kiss of a speaker bringing a killer to a chamber.

He did not speak.

He did not move.

He looked at her with a question in his eyes.

Thirty-Four

She did not stop.

She had been told not to stop, and she did not stop. The instruction held her in a way she had not understood would hold her when Vorathan had given it in the dry air of the east conference room. She kept the carrier. She kept the tones. She kept the glyph rendering on her patch, which had gone pale at the edges because her body was spending more chemistry on the suspension than on the patch, and her patch was the first thing her body was letting go.

The wearing was at its peak.

She knew this because the Thren literature had told her the peak would arrive at fourteen minutes, and she was at fourteen minutes, and the heat along her throat and jaw and wrists had plateaued in a way she could feel if she attended to it, which she did not. She kept her attention on the carrier. The voice was still present. The voice was thin. The voice was, for the moment, enough.

Adrian had not moved.

He was looking at her across the volume. The chamber was looking at him. Dhillon was looking at him.

Halpern-Ødegård was looking at him. Adrian was looking at her. He was not moving. The question in his eyes had settled. The question had become an answer neither of them was going to say aloud.

Nia did not meet his eye.

She had been told, by Vorathan, that the rite did not permit the speaker to look at a caught signature during the answering register, because to do so would register as accusation, and accusation was not the rite's grammar. The rite was finding. The finding was the chamber's. The speaker was the voice of the chamber. The speaker did not accuse.

She looked above him. She let the volume of the chamber hold him.

The answering finished at the sixteenth minute, which was two minutes past the end of the literature's predicted window, and which Nia registered as the rite having run longer for her than it would have run for a Thren of full standing. She had been warned.

The chamber was full of settled responses.

The signature above the human arc, which was Adrian's device's output, was still in the volume, slow-drifting, unmistakable.

Nia understood, standing on the tile island with the wearing at its peak, that the answering was complete, and that the answering was the part of the rite the Thren were present for, and that the next part was hers alone.

She reached for the right pocket.

Her hand was slow. The wearing had thickened her fingers in a way she had not been told to expect, because the literature on the wearing had been written by scholars who had never performed the rite themselves, because the scholars who had performed the rite and had survived had either refused to write about the wearing or had written about it in registers the Concordance library had not acquired. Nia had been warned about the wearing. She had not been warned about the fingers.

Her hand found the felt pouch. Her fingers found the cap of the gold vial. She uncapped it with her thumb, which was a motion she had practiced eighteen times in dry air and which her thumb remembered.

She released the suppressor.

It drifted into the volume of the chamber at the height of her throat, which was where she had been warned to release it for the correct geometry of the closing. The gold spread slowly. Its grammar was to dampen the active response signatures. It did what it was grammared to do.

The chamber dimmed.

She counted three of her beats.

At the third beat she released the held name.

She had, in the fraction of a second before she released it, understood the weight of Vorathan's phrasing, which had been in his private notation: the name of a speaker held against the chamber until the chamber had been answered. The held name was a name one held. She had held it in her pocket for three days. She had held it in her hand for nine seconds. She released it now.

The indigo did not drift. It moved through the chamber in the slow precise pattern of a signature that had been designed to move, and it met every active response signature in the volume, and it closed them. The chamber, which had been full of settled responses and the wearing and Adrian's device's output and Nia's compulsion phrases, went quiet.

The held name settled.

The rite closed.

She did not fall.

She had been prepared, by Vorathan in the second teaching day, for the possibility of falling, which would have required the embassy medical detail to enter the chamber and would have invalidated the closing's final beat and would have been, in the Thren reading, a bad landing. Nia had not practiced not-falling. Not-falling was not a thing you could practice. But she had practiced holding the carrier, and she had practiced holding the carrier while exhausted, and she had, at the end, held enough.

She was not exactly standing. She was resting her weight on the tile island in a way the tile had been shaped to permit, and her legs were shaking, and she was not looking at her legs because the Thren literature said a speaker did not look at her legs during the close of a rite, which she had always read as a Thren quirk and which she now understood as practical instruction.

The first Thren to move was the First-Speaker.

The First-Speaker cycled her three modes in a signature Nia registered, with the slight delay of a body still in the wearing, as the first Thren congratulation a Concordance human had ever received in the full register. The First Current was saying, in chemistry and pigment and vocalization at once, that the rite had been performed correctly. The First Current was saying that the speaker was a speaker.

The Sixth Current followed.

The Second Current followed.

The Fourth Current followed, indigo thin and careful, and Nia understood this as Nemari.

The Seventh did not respond.

Nia did not look for them. She had been told not to.

The suspension began to drain.

It was the same drain she had felt eleven days ago, the slow withdrawal of the medium from the upper volume first, the warmth retreating in a plane across her face and then her shoulders and then her chest. As it withdrew, it took the chemistry with it, which was the point: the chamber was returning to ordinary time. The signatures of the four consenting Currents went out of the volume like a tide. Adrian's device's output, which had been in the upper volume above the human arc, was drawn down into the recovery mantle where, Nia understood with a small precise scholarly satisfaction, it would be preserved in the record.

She had done it.

She did not say so.

She waited until the suspension had fallen to her waist. Then she stepped off the tile island. Her legs carried her. She was surprised that her legs carried her, and she noted the surprise without investigating it, because there would be time to investigate it later.

She walked toward the airlock.

The humans in the arc had been released from their ceremonial posture by the rite's close. Adrian had not moved. Halpern-Ødegård was being spoken to quietly by Dhillon. Ilsia was looking at Nia the way a journalist looked at a story that had just delivered itself. Dhillon looked up, saw Nia walking, and left Halpern-Ødegård mid-sentence. He crossed to the airlock. He met her there.

He did not ask her if she was all right. He offered his arm.

She took it.

They walked out.

Thirty-Five

The medical detail was waiting outside the airlock.

Two corporals and an older woman in the pale-grey of a senior Concordance physician, whom Nia had not met and whose name she did not ask. The older woman took Nia's pulse with two fingers at her wrist, which was, Nia realized with a small scholarly delay, the Thren way of taking a pulse, not the human way, and which was either a deliberate choice or a habit. Nia did not ask. She let the woman take the pulse.

"Doctor," the physician said.

"Yes."

"You are going to the infirmary."

"I am not."

"I am going to write you up going to the infirmary regardless of whether you go."

"I understand. I am not going."

The physician looked at her for a long moment. Then she looked at Dhillon. Dhillon did not say anything. The physician nodded once.

"I will write you up as refusing transport," she said. "I will add a clinical note that you were ambulatory, coherent, and present to your own decision-making. If you change your mind, my comm is routed to the infirmary duty line."

"Thank you."

The physician stepped back. The corporals stepped back. Dhillon offered Nia his arm a second time. She took it.

They walked.

They walked to Dhillon's office. They did not speak on the walk. The compound at the hour after the rite was in a quiet that was not the quiet of before the rite; it was the quiet of a building whose staff had learned that something had happened and were waiting, in the specific professional way Concordance staff waited, for official word of what. Adaeze Okonkwo was not at the junction. Three junior officers were in the corridor to the civil service wing. None of them looked at Nia. All of them registered her.

Dhillon's outer office was empty. He closed the inner door behind them.

He sat her on the bench he kept by the window. He brought her water. He brought her a folded blanket that the civil service had not, in Nia's knowledge, kept in its offices. It was Concordance-issue, soft, and warm in the way a blanket was warm when it had been kept somewhere warm.

"When did you put this in here," Nia said.

"Three days ago."

"You knew."

"I knew the rite would end in this office, if it ended."

"You prepared for that."

"I prepared for that."

"Thank you."

"Doctor."

"Yes."

"Let me tell you what has happened."

Dhillon sat across from her in the chair he rarely sat in. He held a dataslate in his lap the way he held it during formal civil service briefings, which was a tell she had come to read.

"Dr. Cho is in the embassy security wing, in a secured room, under medical observation and standing arrest on a charge of conspiracy to assassinate a Concordance official. The charge was filed by my office within eleven minutes of the rite's close. He has not been formally interviewed. His rights under Concordance criminal procedure have been read to him in three registers. He has asked for counsel. He has not spoken otherwise."

"Halpern-Ødegård."

"Detained. She is in a different secured room. She has been charged with falsification of a Concordance scientific record and with aiding and abetting the act Dr. Cho is charged with. She has invoked her right to counsel. She has also, in the minute between her arrest and her request for counsel, told the arresting officer that she wishes to cooperate."

"Which is a thing she will not remember saying when her counsel arrives."

"It is a thing the arresting officer remembers, and the arresting officer's written record is a Concordance document."

"Good."

"Thirdwater Research."

"Yes."

"The Concordance attorney general's office was briefed during the rite. A preliminary civil filing is in draft. The Concordance will name Thirdwater Research as the institutional actor behind the synthesis of the poison that killed Ambassador Vance. The filing will cite the Kallmann-Iwasaki paper, the dimensions correspondence, the seven-and-thirteen feature asymmetry, and Dr. Halpern-Ødegård's position at Thirdwater in the eight months before her short-rotation assignment. The filing will not name Halcyon Reach."

"No."

"No."

"Because we cannot prove it yet."

"Because we cannot prove it yet."

"How long."

"Longer than this book."

Nia did not ask Dhillon what he meant by this book, because she understood.

"Ilsia Moreau's first dispatch went out to Earth at the seventeenth minute of the rite, which I am told is the fastest dispatch a journalist of her rank has filed in the history of the Sepharu embassy. Her cover register is the apology-to-the-volume, which I had briefed her on before the rite for exactly this eventuality. She will report the rite accurately and quietly. She will report Dr. Cho's arrest as a separate story, which she has been told she may publish in twenty-four hours and which she has agreed to."

"She has agreed to wait."

"She has agreed to wait, because the Chair has asked her to. She is morally gray. She is not morally foolish."

"All right."

"The Chair is awake. She was briefed during the rite and is currently in conversation with the Parliament's standing committee on Sepharu affairs. I do not yet know the outcome of that conversation. I expect to know within the hour."

Nia nodded.

She was, she realized somewhere near the end of Dhillon's sentence, holding the water with both hands because one hand would have shaken.

Dhillon set the slate down.

"There is one more thing."

"Yes."

"The Chair, in the second minute of her conversation with the standing committee, informed the committee that she intends to ratify, as a field appointment, your promotion to Principal Envoy of the Sepharu delegation. The ratification is not yet final. It will be final by the end of the Chair's working day, which is to say in about two hours. I want you to know before it reaches you through a Concordance press release."

"Principal Envoy."

"Principal Envoy."

"Dhillon."

"Doctor."

"I am thirty-one."

"Yes."

"Principal Envoys are not thirty-one."

"No. You will be the first one who is. The Chair has anticipated the objection. She has responded with the argument that the Thren have already accepted you as a speaker of family-level standing, which is a standing the Concordance does not typically assign to Principal Envoys and which, the Chair has pointed out, no other Concordance staffer currently holds."

"She is using the Thren to appoint me."

"She is using what the Thren have done to argue for an appointment she already wanted to make."

"Why."

"Because Sepharu is going to need an envoy who can do what you just did, and there is no one else available who can. Also because, I suspect, she likes how you have handled the last eleven days."

"I have not handled the last eleven days."

"You have handled them enough that the Chair wants you in the position. That is what handling them means in her register."

Nia drank from the water.

"I do not want the job," she said.

"I know."

"I am going to take it."

"I know."

"Thank you for the blanket."

"Doctor."

"I am going to go to my quarters. I am going to sleep. If the Chair ratifies the appointment, I will come to this office tomorrow at oh nine hundred and I will accept it properly. If she does not, I will come at oh nine hundred anyway."

"All right."

"Dhillon."

"Yes."

"Adrian."

"He is in the security wing. He will be transferred to Earth on the next gate rotation, which is in five days. You can visit him any time before then."

"Okay."

"Doctor."

"I will visit him tomorrow."

She stood. She handed the water back. She kept the blanket around her shoulders. She walked to the door.

Dhillon did not stand up.

"I am glad you are alive," he said.

She did not turn back. She nodded at the door. She walked out.

Thirty-Six

She went to see Adrian at oh nine thirty.

The security wing was on the third sub-level, two corridors down from the medical wing. She had been required to pass through three separate access checks to reach the room where he was being held. The checks were not hostile; they were procedural, performed by corporals who knew who she was and had been briefed on the fact that a visit from the Principal Envoy-designate to the arrested exobiologist was going to happen and was going to happen at the hour she had set. They had arranged chairs. They had a recording device in the ceiling and another on the table. They had given her a note explaining what the recordings would be used for. She had read the note. She had signed it.

The door opened.

Adrian was sitting at the table.

He looked thinner. That was the first thing. He had been thin when he had come to her quarters three nights ago and he was thinner now, which could have been the overnight loss of a man who had not slept, or could have been the particular hollowing of a man who had been told, in a formal civil service register, that the rest of his life had just been arranged without him.

She sat down across from him.

He did not speak. She did not speak. A full minute passed.

"Nee," he said.

"Adrian."

"They told me you were coming."

"I said I was coming."

"I was not sure until the door opened."

"I am here."

"Yes."

She had been advised, by Dhillon, that a visit to Adrian would go one of three ways: he would refuse to speak, he would speak and lie, or he would speak and tell the truth. Dhillon had said he thought Adrian would speak and tell the truth. Nia had not believed Dhillon. Nia had been wrong.

"Why," she said.

Adrian closed his eyes for a moment. He did not rehearse what he was going to say. She registered this. She had been waiting to register it.

"My sister," he said.

"Your sister."

"My sister has four children and a husband who is not well and a husband's mother who is not well. They live in Lagos, on Earth. They have lived in Lagos since my sister decided, at twenty, that she was not going off-world. She runs a small firm that sells Thren-derived atmospheric science to Terran climate clients. It is a small firm. It employs nine people. My sister is the reason they employ nine people."

"Adrian."

"Let me tell you this."

"Tell me."

"Fourteen months ago a Halcyon Reach intermediary came to my sister's firm with a research partnership offer. The terms were attractive. She accepted. The partnership dissolved three months later. In the dissolution, two of her firm's contracts with Terran climate clients were found to have been, quietly, the intermediary's own portfolio. Her firm was left holding obligations it could not meet. She lost the two contracts. She lost three others in the next quarter, because in the Terran climate sector a firm that has been found to have been holding another firm's obligations is a firm the market does not want. Her firm shrank to four employees."

"Seven months ago her oldest child, who is six, was diagnosed with a medical condition that required treatment in a Concordance-certified Terran facility. The Concordance insurance line covered the initial review. The appeal line, which governs covered treatments, held the treatment in review. The review has been in review for seven months. My sister has been paying out of pocket, which she cannot do, for six of those seven months."

"Three months ago a Halcyon Reach intermediary came to my sister with an offer. The offer was a grant to her firm that would restore it to its previous size, plus a personal medical line that would clear her son's treatment through the appeal queue. The grant had no terms. The medical line had no terms. The intermediary said it was a gesture of goodwill, from a firm that had appreciated the partnership even though the partnership had not worked out."

"Your sister did not take the offer."

"She did not take the offer. She is my sister. She is careful."

"The intermediary came back."

"The intermediary came to me. In the compound."

"When."

"Four months ago. Three weeks before I arrived at Sepharu."

"In the compound at the Academy."

"At the Academy. I met him in a coffee shop two streets over. He knew where I was going. He knew I was going to Sepharu. He knew Vance was going to be there. He had a complete file on my work history, which I had not, at that point, made available to Halcyon Reach in any register. He had a complete file on my sister's firm. He had, in a separate folder, a schedule of the Concordance insurance appeal line's typical rejection patterns for her son's condition. He did not threaten me. He did not need to. He asked me if I would consider consulting, in my private capacity, on a chemistry problem Halcyon Reach's research wing was working on. He said the consultation would be small. He said it would be private. He said, at the end, that his firm had a continuing interest in the well-being of my sister's family."

"And you consulted."

"I consulted."

"On the chemistry that killed Vance."

"I did not know it would kill Vance. I believed, for about nine weeks, that I was consulting on a research problem about suspension-adjacent chemistry. I understood on the tenth week what the research problem was for. By then I had been consulting for two months. By then the intermediary had made a second visit, which had included the information that my sister's son's appeal had, coincidentally, cleared the review queue on the day of the first consultation. My sister had been paid by a grant she did not know my employer had made. My sister had her firm back."

"You did not tell her."

"I did not tell her."

"Adrian."

"I am telling you."

Nia sat with this.

She did not forgive him. She had not come here to forgive him, and she had known she would not, and she did not. What she did, instead, was register the shape of what he was telling her the way she registered any shape of language: with the trained attention of a linguist reading a register she had not been taught but could parse.

He was telling her the truth.

He was telling her the truth because he had decided, somewhere between the moment the chamber had caught him and the moment she had opened the door this morning, that the truth was the thing he had left. He had lost his career. He had lost his standing. He had lost her, in every register in which she had ever been his. The truth was the only thing the intermediary had not, eventually, been able to trade away from him. He was telling her because he had nothing else to offer.

She understood this.

She did not forgive him.

"Adrian."

"Nee."

"I am going to leave."

"All right."

"I am not going to ask you anything else."

"All right."

"I will not come back."

He looked at her.

"Nee."

"Yes."

"Tell my sister."

"I will not tell your sister."

"Someone has to tell her what happened."

"Someone will. It will not be me."

"All right."

"Adrian."

"Yes."

"The tea was very thoughtful of you."

He closed his eyes.

She stood.

She did not touch him. She did not say goodbye. She walked to the door, tapped the release panel, and the corporal opened it. She walked out into the corridor.

She walked back to her quarters.

She did not cry in the corridor.

She did not cry on the elevator.

She did not cry at her door.

She went inside. She closed the door. She sat at the desk for a long moment. Then she stood up, and she crossed to the galley alcove, and she opened the tin of tea he had sent her three weeks before the rite. She boiled water. She made a cup. She drank it.

It was the tea she had liked at twenty-four.

She drank the whole cup.

She did not make a second.

Thirty-Seven

Vorathan's message came on the afternoon of the second day after the rite.

It arrived through the embassy monitoring portal, not through her comm, which Nia understood as a choice and which she registered with the small scholarly note she had come to keep for her readings of him. He had, once again, spoken to her through a system Concordance officers above her rank did not routinely examine. He had, once again, respected the architecture of their correspondence.

The message was short.

It said: my Current has decided. I am permitted to see you. Meet me in the lesser chamber at sixteen hundred.

Nia did not reply. She did not need to. She walked to the lesser chamber at fifteen forty-eight, without an escort, because the compound had, on the morning after the rite, quietly ended her confinement and quietly reassigned the junior officers who had walked her corridors for eleven days. Dhillon had sent her a note about the reassignment and she had not replied to that either. She had not yet decided what to do with the freedom.

She entered the lesser chamber's airlock at fifteen fifty-six.

She cycled the inner door.

Vorathan was in the chamber.

He was in the posture of attending at an angle, not the formal posture of a Fourth Current scholar on official business, which was the posture he had held at the First-Speaker's ruling. The difference was small and was meant for her. He was telling her, without words, that this meeting was between them.

She crossed to the tile island. She stood.

His signature was lighter than she had read it in the last two weeks. The tightness was not entirely gone; she did not expect it to be entirely gone for a while. But it had loosened at the edges in the way a signature loosened when a speaker had been held in review and had come out of it on their feet.

"Iyana."

"Vorathan."

"My Current has decided."

"Tell me."

"The Current has concluded that my actions in the matter of your rite were consistent with the rite's outcome. The rite performed correctly. The rite found what it was called to find. The Current has decided that the rite's correctness is, in the Current's philosophical register, the correct measure of my actions. I have been exonerated."

Nia let out a breath she had not known she was holding.

"However."

"Yes."

"The Current has also concluded that I acted without the Current's permission when I taught you the closing, when I synthesized the suppressor and the held name for you, and when I released the chemical signature into the garden on the day of your first petition. These were correct actions. They were also, strictly, acts of a scholar speaking for his Current without the Current's authorization. The Current has decided that actions that are correct but unauthorized are actions that require a small formal cost, both because the Current must say it is the Current, and because a scholar who believes he may act correctly without authorization is a scholar who will, in time, act incorrectly without authorization."

"Yes."

"I am on Current probation for one Thren year. I may continue my scholarship. I may continue my correspondence with you. I may not speak in Current affairs. I may not attend Current councils. I may not co-sign papers of Fourth Current standing. At the end of the year the Current will lift the probation. Nemari has been assigned as the reviewing scholar."

"Nemari."

"Nemari. Who has, I am told, indicated to the Current that she has reconsidered her position on your rite in the light of the rite's outcome. She will not say she was wrong. The Thren do not say they were wrong. She has, in her own register, said it."

"All right."

"Vorathan."

"Yes."

"A year."

"A Thren year. Twenty of your months."

"That is a long time."

"It is a year. It will end. I have what I had."

"You have less."

"I have less. I have enough."

He cycled a small phrase in his chemical register, three features and a trailing beat, a compound idiom Nia did not know. She translated it roughly in her head as what falls between two readings, and was not confident of the translation. She did not ask him for a better one. He had not offered.

He was, she registered, not asking her to be sorry. He was telling her the shape of what had happened and expecting her to receive it the way he had received the Current's ruling, which was to say without apology and without complaint. She did what he was expecting.

"Thank you," she said.

"For what."

"For the teaching. For the vials. For the year."

He did not answer immediately.

"You are welcome for the teaching and the vials," he said. "The year is not mine to give you."

"The Seventh."

"Yes."

"Was the young Thren real."

Vorathan was quiet for a longer moment than she had expected.

"I cannot tell you with the certainty you want," he said. "I can tell you what I have since learned. The First-Speaker received the Seventh's consent at oh seven that morning in a register that is not documented in any Concordance source and that my Current has, in the last two days, told me exists. The Seventh Current uses a transmission mode that goes through the body of another speaker, at that speaker's moment of altered state. The Thren call it the shared speaking. It is not possession. It is not hallucination. It is the Seventh using a speaker's own voice, for a measured instant, to say a thing the Seventh needs said. The speaker remembers it as their own speaking. The Seventh remembers it as their own. The distinction between the two is not one the Thren have ever found a grammar for, and it is not one I am likely to resolve for you today."

"The young Thren."

"Was either you speaking the Seventh's question to yourself, in a mode you had opened by being in the third interval, or the Seventh speaking through you, in the mode they use for this. Or, and this is the third possibility my Current has considered, a junior Seventh scholar was physically in your quarters for six minutes in a register I am not permitted to describe. I do not know which of the three happened. I think it was not the third. I cannot tell you which of the first two it was."

"That is not an answer."

"It is the answer I have. The Seventh does not give closer answers."

"All right."

She was quiet for a long moment.

"I am Principal Envoy," she said.

"I heard. Congratulations."

"Thank you."

"Iyana."

"Yes."

"I will see you again. I will see you more often than a Fourth Current scholar on probation ought to see a Concordance Principal Envoy. My Current has not prohibited that, which I consider a small private grace."

"Good."

"I will not be in the audience chamber for any ceremony that matters to the Currents for a year."

"I will."

"I know."

"Vorathan."

"Yes."

"I am glad you are still here."

"I am glad you are still here."

He cycled his three modes in a signature she now recognized on sight, because she had felt it once before, in the east conference room on the last teaching day: the signature the Thren used between speakers who had been through a rite together and were agreeing, without saying so, to that fact.

She returned it as best she could, in human gesture and in the glyph her patch still carried. She did not get it right. He did not correct her, but he smiled. The attempt was the point.

She stepped back from the tile island. She cycled the airlock. She walked out of the lesser chamber into the dry air of the corridor.

She walked back through the compound toward her new quarters.

Thirty-Eight

The new quarters overlooked the audience chamber.

That was the first thing she noticed, at twenty-one oh seven on the evening of the second day after the rite, when the embassy's residential staff had finished moving the last of her possessions into the Principal Envoy's residence on the upper level of the compound. She had asked the staff to leave her the final placement of things herself, because there were things the staff would not have known how to place. They had left. She had unpacked at her own pace, which was slow, because the wearing was still with her in specific places and the pace her body was willing to set was not the pace she would have set a week ago.

The quarters were larger. They had a small library alcove, which was a practical consideration of the Concordance envoy track and which she had not expected to register as a gift. They had a galley with a working sonic dishwasher. They had a bedroom separated from the main room by a half-wall the embassy designers had chosen to render in a color called late-afternoon stone. They had a window.

The window looked down into the audience chamber.

It was a one-way glass. The chamber's staff could not see the Principal Envoy's residence from inside. The Principal Envoy could see the chamber. The chamber was not in use at this hour. Its suspension had been drained and was being cycled through its weekly recovery, which was a thing the Concordance had never been permitted to observe until last year and which, Nia now understood, was also a thing the Concordance Principal Envoy was permitted to observe from her residence as a matter of course. The lights in the chamber ran on a gentle rotation the embassy had calibrated for cycle. They shifted through the amber-green spectrum at a pace slower than a human breath.

She stood at the window.

She had opened the tin of tea Adrian had sent her on the morning of the first day. She had drunk one cup. She had not drunk a second. She had not thrown the tin away. The tin was on the counter in the galley. She would drink the rest of it over the next year, or she would not. She did not know which she would do, and she did not need to decide tonight.

Adrian was, as of this morning's Concordance press release, being transferred to Earth on the next gate rotation to face trial. Halpern-Ødegård had, in the three hours after her arrest, begun to cooperate in a register her counsel had not yet been able to contain. Thirdwater Research had, within the hour of Ilsia's second dispatch, closed its public offices and referred all inquiries to a corporate attorney who was, Dhillon had told her, already being prepared as a witness for the Concordance. Halcyon Reach's name had not yet appeared in any press release. Nia expected it would, eventually. She had written in her private notes that she would look for it, and that she would know it when it came, and that she would be the person the Concordance came to when it came, because she was now the Principal Envoy, and because the Principal Envoy was a person the Concordance came to when things had names.

The silence Adrian had left was the silence of a friend who had not died, which was a worse silence than the silence of a friend who had.

She registered this.

She registered it with the small specific attention she had always paid to the registers of silence.

She stood at the window.

She was afraid.

She was afraid in a way she had been refusing to be afraid for eleven days, because the eleven days had not permitted the fear, and her body had not asked for the fear, and the work had required her to put the fear aside. The work was done. She was Principal Envoy. She was thirty-one years old. She had opened a Thren mourning rite and closed it correctly. She had caught the man who had killed her mentor with her own kiss. She had been consented to by four Currents of a species she had been writing papers about since twenty-two. She was, as of this evening, the most senior living Concordance human who had ever performed a Thren rite.

She was afraid of everything that was going to happen next.

She was afraid of the Concordance trial. She was afraid of the people above Adrian who had not yet been caught. She was afraid of what she would have to do to find them. She was afraid of the year Vorathan was going to be on probation, and she was afraid, though less, of the year after. She was afraid of the body that had survived the wearing, because the body had survived the wearing and the scholars who had survived the wearing had come out of it different, and she did not yet know in what way she had come out of it different, and she did not know how long it would take to find out.

She was afraid.

She let herself be afraid.

She stood at the window for a long time.

The suspension's lights moved through their slow cycle in the chamber below. She watched them move. She did not cry. She did not look away. She let her hand rest against the glass, which was cool, which was glass and not something else. The glass reminded her where she was.

She was a speaker who had come out of a rite the way the rite sent speakers out. She was a person who had loved someone and had brought him to the chamber. She was a Principal Envoy. She was a daughter of two cryptographers and a session musician, under the legal kinship of Earth. She was standing in her quarters on Sepharu at the end of the second day of the seventh month of the twenty-second year, which was the year she would remember later, if she remembered years at all, as the year she had become what she was going to be.

She did not know what that was.

She was going to find out.

Enjoy an excerpt from

Seven Currents

Book Two of The Envoy Chronicles

Available May 15, 2026

One

The light on Luna was a light Nia had once loved, and she was trying to love it again. The Academy's north reading room kept its winter lamps on through the long lunar morning: a bank of warm sun-coded panels above the shelves that corrected the window's real, colder wedge, so that a human mind on a long day of reading would not be reminded at the edge of its vision that true sunrise was still six hours out. The dome's canned air smelled of almost nothing. It was the almost that Nia noticed now. Paper, a little. Warm wood from the study carrels. The clean metal trace of a filtered vent. A Thren year on Sepharu, six weeks on Luna, and she still woke every morning into the wrong air.

She sat at the corner table with her back to the window, a notebook open in front of her, a fountain pen in her hand, and nothing she trusted to put down. Across the room a first-year she did not know was folded into a carrel, reading something on a tablet and not looking up. In the galley across the corridor someone was making tea in the slow deliberate way people made tea when they did not want to finish it and be alone in the next hour. Nia understood. She had come down from her quarters early for the same reason.

The Academy had given her its guest seat for the term. Six weeks in the junior scholars' wing: a seminar of eleven doctoral candidates, a reading room with a window onto the long dawn, three afternoon debriefs a week with the civil service officers who were trying to write the official account of the ninth day in a language the High Parliament could read without moving. The seminar she had enjoyed. The candidates were serious, and one of them had been almost rude to her in the first session, which had told her more about the candidate than the candidate had meant to share, and which she had liked. The debriefs she had not enjoyed. This afternoon was the last of them. She had allowed herself to think of afternoon as the interior of a shell she would step out of at about sixteen hundred local, after which the rest of the week was hers, and after that the rest of the term, and after that a shuttle back.

She did not, this morning, feel that she owned any of those hours.

The galley attendant brought her a cup of tea without being asked. He was a student staffer, thin in the lunar way, and he set the cup on the coaster with the small care of someone who had registered, without looking at her face, that she was not an easy morning. He did not say anything. Nia nodded once, which he received, and he went back to the galley. She wrapped her hands around the cup. It was thirty seconds too hot. She kept her hands on it anyway. On Sepharu the compound's small galley had been too narrow to sit in; she had taken her morning tea standing at a window above the north bay, and had walked with it, still burning, through the corridor to her desk. She had done this every morning for a Thren year, a small habit of standard atmosphere, of being able to hold a warm thing. Inside the suspension the warmth would have dispersed into the medium before it reached her hands, and a Thren would have read the dispersion as speech;

which was why the habit mattered, why she had kept it carefully separate from her hours in the suspension, why it belonged to the part of her Sepharu day that had been, of all things, private. The habit had come with her to Luna. She had not, in six weeks, been able to put it down.

She had written a line across the top of the notebook an hour ago and had not written anything under it. The line read, in her own small hand: for the seminar, a paragraph on silence. She had meant to open the last session on the First Current's withdrawal after the murder, on the textbook distinction between the half-beat and the speech that will not be spoken, and to let the candidates work at it. She could do the session without the paragraph. She had taught the chapter four times. But the paragraph was the thing she had wanted to leave them with, and this morning no paragraph would come.

She thought of what her own professor had said about teaching, in a seminar Nia would remember in the specific way one remembered lines from ceremonies. Obi-Halloran had said: the sentence you cannot finish on the page is usually the sentence that is doing the most work. Leave the space and come back to it. Nia had left the space. The space had been waiting six weeks.

She wrote, very neatly, under the line: silence is not one thing.

Then she closed the notebook.

The door at the far end of the reading room opened, and a draft moved through, the light lunar draft that never felt right to a station-raised body, too dry, not slow enough. Obi-Halloran herself came through the door with her coat over her arm and her hair shorter than Nia remembered. She lifted her free hand in the gesture their doctoral cohort had used for hello during the long quiet hours of general examinations, two fingers up and the thumb laid flat, and she crossed to the table with the unhurried gait of a woman who had decided to take her tea here and not at the senior table today. She sat. She did not ask. She set her coat on the chair next to her and looked at the cup in Nia's hands and said, without any inflection that required a reply, "Too hot yet."

Nia said, "Thirty seconds."

"I'll wait with you," Obi-Halloran said.

They sat. Obi-Halloran pulled her own cup toward her, which a member of the galley staff had already produced at her elbow without a signal Nia had caught, and she did not drink either. They had sat together like this twice during the term, both times unplanned, both times in silence that was not unfriendly. Nia had not, in six weeks, told her former teacher anything about the ninth day that Obi-Halloran could not read in the official account, and Obi-Halloran had not asked.

Nia's terminal chimed.

The tone was the Concordance diplomatic service's three-note descending sequence: not urgent, not classified, confirm receipt within the hour. It was a tone she had heard every day for a Thren year on Sepharu and perhaps twice on Luna. Her body recognized it before her mind did. She set the tea down a little too hard, and the cup rang against the table. Across from her Obi-Halloran's eyes dropped to the cup once and came back up, and did not ask.

Nia turned the terminal over.

The message had come through Dhillon's handle on the Sepharu delegation's channel, routed instant through the gate, timestamped twelve minutes earlier. The subject line read, in the civil service's flat standard font: FIRST

CURRENT — SUCCESSION — RETURN REQUESTED.

Nia read the body once. Then she read it again.

The First-Speaker, the message said, had completed her speaking in the small hours of Sepharu local. The phrasing was Dhillon's careful translation of what the First Current had delivered to the compound at oh two forty-five by suspension courier: the First-Speaker has set her speech down. She had been unwell for a Thren month, which the compound had not been formally told. She had named no successor aloud, which was within her right. The succession was open. The First Current had entered ritual silence. The Second Current had already, within three hours, requested a formal consultation with the human delegation. The Third Current had requested isolation. The Fourth Current had said nothing at all. Dhillon's own note, appended, was four lines: the Acting Principal Envoy has the compound until your return. I have held the Second Current's request at receipt-confirmed without reply. A berth has been held for you on the 14:20 Luna-to-gate shuttle this afternoon; an onward transit to Sepharu orbit is available at gate-time plus four. Come when you can.

Nia put the terminal down. Across the table Obi-Halloran had not moved, but her hands had rearranged themselves around her cup in the way a person rearranged their hands when they had decided not to ask.

"She's dead," Nia said. It was the plainest possible translation, and her mouth chose it. "The First-Speaker."

Obi-Halloran closed her eyes for a long breath and opened them. "When."

"Oh two forty-five their time."

"The Currents."

"Silence. Isolation. Nothing at all. A consultation request from the Second." She heard herself name the responses in the textbook order and did not correct herself. The order was the order of the textbook because it was the order the Thren used. "I'm being called back."

"Of course you are," Obi-Halloran said.

Nia looked down at her own hands. They looked like her hands. Adrian had held one of them, two mornings before his transfer, in the small secured chamber where she had gone to say a last thing and had not said it. She thought of him and then did not think of him. Adrian was not her hands. The First-Speaker was her hands. The First-Speaker had been the one to fold her three channels into a posture Nia had not known, in the minute after Vance had fallen; the First-Speaker had been the silver-green of the ninth day, the voice in her teeth, the patience under weight. Nia had not seen her since. The last image Nia had of her was from the suspension's own recording, a Thren standing in the upper volume with her signature pulled close against her body, every color in the room dying around her.

"I don't know," Nia said, to her hands, "whether I grieve her. I want to say I do. I knew her voice. I don't know that I knew her."

"You grieve her voice," Obi-Halloran said. "Grieve the voice. The rest will sort itself on the gate."

Nia lifted her head. "I have a session at fifteen hundred."

"I'll take it."

"It's the silence session."

"I know what session it is," Obi-Halloran said, mildly. "I taught it to you. Go pack."

Nia packed.

The scholar's room in the junior wing was a small room, and she had lived in it lightly. The bed made itself under a hand-pass of the sheet; the shelves carried six books she had brought and one she had bought; her clothes folded into the single soft case she traveled with. At the bottom of the case, under the folded clothes, she set the small hard case that held her vials: twenty-three glass stubs in padded slots, each keyed in her private notation to a single phrase, cleared for scholarly transport under the Concordance's cross-species research protocols and carried by her through customs on three planets. She had not opened the case in six weeks. She lifted it once to check the latch and set it down, and as she set it down her hand rested on it a moment longer than a check required. It was the heaviest thing she was taking back.

She sent two messages before she closed her terminal. The first was to Dhillon: receipt confirmed; on the 14:20. The second was to Adaeze Okonkwo at the Sepharu compound's administrative desk, three lines in civil-service neutral, asking for a quiet return. No reception on the pad. No public routing through the atrium. Adaeze would know what to do with it. Adaeze had been the one to process Nia's arrival papers a Thren year before, and had given her, at that desk, the small wordless recognition two women gave each other when they shared a second language. Nia did not know, this morning, what she would say to Adaeze on the other end. She only knew she wanted the pad to be small.

The gate-transit officer at the Luna shuttleport was a young man in a service jacket who checked her diplomatic standing against the manifest, handed her a boarding chit, and told her in the rote cadence of someone who said it four hundred times a day that Sepharu orbit local time would be late afternoon on arrival. Nia thanked him. She did not ask him whether he had ever stood in a suspension. He had not. His hands were the wrong color for it.

The shuttle climbed out of the dome on the long slow thrust the lunar ascent used, gentle, almost hesitant. Luna fell away below the port in the close pale way a body fell when one had never quite believed one could leave it. Nia watched until the dome's lamps resolved into a single cold point and then closed her eyes. The cabin was half full. The air was thin and clean, scentless, inert. Under her feet, somewhere in the belly of the shuttle, the small hard case of vials sat in her bag with its latch seated, and in one of the slots was a stub keyed to a phrase she had not yet had the courage to translate into English. The phrase, in Thren, was closer to patience under weight than to anything else she knew. She had carried it across two planets and a posting, and she had not, in six weeks on Luna, been able to put it on a page.

She was going back.

Through the port the gate was already a faint green thread above the horizon, and the shuttle's drift was aligning to it. Somewhere ahead of her, past the gate, past the slow drop into Sepharu orbit, past the landing pad the compound kept for diplomatic arrivals, the First Current was in silence, the Second Current was waiting, the rest of the Currents were doing what they did. Someone she had not yet met was already inside the compound, walking the corridors she had walked for a Thren year, learning the way the doors stuck in the winter hour. She did not know the someone's name yet. Dhillon had not put it in the message. She understood, in the small practical way a diplomat understood the shape of a room before she entered it, that the someone would be on the pad when she landed: an attaché, a military post, an introduction she would make standing up, one hand in the listening-to-learn.

The shuttle lifted toward the gate. Nia rested her hand on the case at her hip, and she kept her eyes closed until the chime sounded for the crossing.

www.ingramcontent.com/pod-product-compliance
Lightning Source LLC
LaVergne TN
LVHW010651110826
845149LV00014B/3038